I Gatecrashed Al Pa
A Random Ant

By

GSR Bear

Published 2020

This book is dedicated to my Mum

Index

WARNING!

Under no circumstances are the contents of this book to be taken seriously. All odd essays are, although genuine musings, just for fun. Please return to your soup.

Introduction

What is this book about? Well that's a good question. Perhaps it isn't about anything, or maybe it's about everything? What it is, is a collection of stuff all produced by one person. Who is that person? Well they are named on the cover and in the book itself. For the purposes of this book they have chosen to go by two names.

GSR Bear and the Kosmic Klown.

Neither of these people are real. The person who wrote, drew and edited all the stuff in this book has a name, an actual proper name given at birth.

Does it matter that this name, this real name, isn't being used for this book? Not really, it's all the same stuff whatever, they've decided to call themselves.

So, what's this book about? It's stories, poetry, wacky anecdotes, odd essays and pictures. Some of the stories are funny some are sad. There's science fiction, fantasy, crime drama, as well as a little romance. There's even a nearly forty-year-old comic strip!

I suppose the best thing to do would be to give it a little read. There's an index at the front and you can use this to look up the various entries and find them in the book.

There's no continuity to speak of, all the entries are entirely random, just like the title suggests.

There's no onus on reading it in order, any order that may be apparent is purely coincidental. So just jump in wherever you like.
The random drawings scattered throughout were made for a book I never got paid for so I thought I might as well use them here.

If you enjoy it leave a review ,if don't enjoy it, Well, we don't care that much so you can fuck off. Please return to your soup.

Born an Owl

I was Born at a very early age, under suspicious circumstances, in the back of a Robin Reliant. I was quickly brought up by owls in the wild and after bashing my face in, following only a dozen or so attempts to fly,

I had eventually to leave the nest as the other young owls would deride my inability to swivel my head around 360 degrees. So I made my way out into the world, with only a mild fear of hawks, to find joy and a love of Jam. The Jam was easy, the joy came a little harder. Naaarg! And there's the joy, it came eventually.

It's not an easy world for a young man who thinks he's a very long owl. Many a year were spent trying desperately to be owlish. Roosting (do owls roost?) in trees, I'd fall out all the time. And hunting, I tried hunting voles, mice and the like just as my mentor, Brown, had taught. I was to swoop out of the trees like a mighty talon of vengeance.

Alas yet again, my un-owl like form let me down still further and there was more falling out of trees.

Eventually reason, and my person'ness, prevailed. There was no choice but to embrace my humanity so I joined the rat race, immediately became confused and ran back to the woods.

After which ensued more falling out of trees. It was no good, I was going to have to rethink the whole situation. Lateral thought was needed so I lay down on the ground. At once it hit me, the ground, so, more falling then.

At the same time an idea struck, I was what? I was an owl trapped in a human body. So I got myself a pair of huge round spectacles, and I flew, well flapped my arms, whilst hopping, jumping and running, off to the circus. Where I became the amazing Human Owl! Marvel at his inability to sit on a branch. Go "Ooooo" as he hits the dirt. Mmmmm, I thought, my life to date seems to be developing a bit of a theme?

Ok so I'd been brought up as an owl. An owl, who couldn't fly, roost, (are we still on the fence, as it were, with the owls roosting or not?) hunt or swoop. But what was I good at? I sat on an inconvenient log, to ruminate over my predicament. What could, I do, what oh what could I do? The question would spin around and around my head.

Unlike my actual head which continued to be disappointingly stiff and Intransigent stuck in its 180 degrees, what oh what was I good at though?
"THERE MUST BE SOMETHING?" I thought in capitals.
And then suddenly, it came like a deafening brilliant light, with the taste of diamonds.

I knew my purpose, I knew what I could do. So, after only a brief stint as a superhero, " The Intransigent Owl-Man" I went to Hollywood and became a stuntman. I had found somewhere being able to fall down was a marketable skill and I lived averagely ever after.

The End.

6

Mother

I was really lucky with the one I got,
She's really great you see,
She loves me unconditionally,
And's been very good to me,

I hope you had a good one,
If you didn't then I'm sorry,
Good ones are invaluable,
They never let you worry.

Every creature has a mother,
every bee and bird and bat,
Without them there'd be nobody,
With which to have a chat.

Words

I love words, there's nothing more powerful than words, no gun, nor bomb in fact no weapon made by man has the strength of words. The right words, put together in the right way can change a life.

There are words for all occasions, to suit all needs. Hopes can be raised or dashed, with a single well- chosen sentence. You can be made to feel with words. Words can make you cry, laugh, sing, hate, love and try. Words keenly struck and forged in a mouth, can cut like the sharpest edge. A mind can be changed; thoughts reprogrammed. A life style can be bent and twisted. Words are lies and they are truth.

I like words, they can start wars, and they can end them. They are the expression of all we tell the world we are, what we want people to believe of us, and what we think of others and ourselves. They tell our tales, they enrich our lives. They also repress us. Words are dangerous and they are safe, they are overused and forbidden. They offend and they delight. Words and their creation, their very existence is the utter expression of the dichotomy of what it is to be a feeling thinking human being. Then there's thought, what of thought, I think in words, don't you? Of course you do, so what came first thought, abstraction of self, or words? Descartes, now there was a wordsmith, postulated Cogito ergo sum; I think there for I am. Perhaps illic es lacuna ergo Cogito; there are words therefore I think, may be more appropriate?

So complex are words, that they are different all over the world, and yet they mean the same things, Kibinakh; Ngo oi nei; Je t'dore; Ich liebe dich; Ti voglio bene; GamuSHa; all these words are different but they tell someone they are loved, this gift, this language is the greatest tool the human race possesses. I'm lucky enough to have learnt the words of more than one place in the world, but I've been in places where my words are not understood. There are, I'm sure, many of you, my non-readers, who have felt this loss of power, because that is what it is that comes with the inability to communicate; a total loss of power.

Words are used to make us believe, Hitler used words to drive an entire nation to hate and persecute with no justification. Words can make a fiction out of reality, and truth out of dreams. They are shocking cunt! They are soft pussy, and they are proper vagina. A single word can cause more and longer lasting pain, that a plethora of slaps to the face. They motivate, and they (a cautionary note for the pedants of my non-readership, I've made this next word up) Apathivate (I didn't like de-motivate, it's far too clumsy).

They are our power, and our weakness. They bring us together and they pull us apart. A wise and thoughtful person will learn as many of them as they can, and use them astutely. They can save you as well as damn you.

I love words, and so I hope, do you.

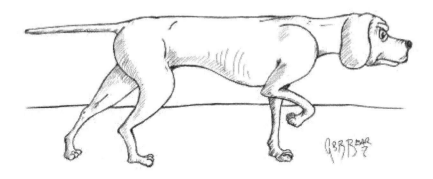

Without Doubt

Without Doubt, what is a man?
Scepticism, assured securer.
Who, without reserve, will believe what they can?
Heeded thy words, my, erstwhile teacher.

Without doubt, what good is belief?
The pain, of falling, for every lie,
Gullibility fools, without relief,
A life in the dark, to escape will we try.

Without doubt, would there be truth?
Move we must, to know all,
Driven, we become, the amateur sleuth,
Guarded be, else beguilingly trapped in thrall.

But what of doubt, and felt, excessively?
Closing in walls around your heart,
Would not this folly destroy sincerity?
Please, oh please, remain open at least in part.

The Love house

New Year's Eve. It's a funny one, I've seen, well, fifty-two of them now. I generally maintain that despite the very probably, extremely disordered state of my brain, I remember everything, but not necessarily in the correct order.

This claim aside, do I really remember all fifty-two New Year's Eves? I don't know. I can, however, remember some with great, what I believe to be, clarity. Is it real? I remember at times, in my youth, experimenting with different states of mind. Quite often I would experiment this way at New Year.

In fact I did on the Eve of 1989 decide, after already having made two, that I would be so altered every New Year for at least the whole of the next decade, I made it with three years on top of that.

Though you may get my point, there are no doubt many among my non-readership that will be thinking, something like:

"Well then, in that case I can't believe anything you say!"

Ok then, stop not reading now;

Have they gone? They have? Ok then, so you know what I mean, my non-readers, I have wonderful clarity that allows me to recognise that there sometimes exists a subtle line between recollection and imagination; in fact both functions exist in the same place in the brain.

But memory is all about the noises and imagery, memory is pictures and sounds, and that's where the clarity lies: in the sense of it all. Some things are so clear I often doubt they happened at all. Like the New Year's Eve I spent with friends at the "Love House" on 31st December 1990.

I watched this particular New Year begin in Camden, in London, with, among others, my friend, I'll call her Crystal Tips, she knows who she is and that's all that matters. We drove to London, the Boatman, Zira, me and another, arriving only just in time for midnight.

11

We parked up and leapt into a pub, just to allow us the chance to Auld Lang Syne with other humans. So, with traditional New Year bon ami and crossed arms we were accepted by smiling strangers into a circle of the singing.

Then it was off to find Crystal Tips in a pub, which we did, surprisingly quickly, and after much dancing on tables and bars, came last orders and time at the bar. We found ourselves, with our numbers swelled, once more on the street.

"Where to next?" I enquired of my London friends.

"To the Love House," was the reply.

My travelling companions and I could only wonder what this could be.

"Oh Kosmic, (she of course used my real name, there was no Kosmic Klown in those days) it's the most marvellous place full of fun and frivolity!" Was Crystal Tips's reply.

After a short walk we arrived at the "Love House", and she was right. It was indeed a most marvellous place. It was a squat, an enormous vacant London town house, now occupied by a number of creative types. I'll never know if I met the actual occupants or not. But I did, never the less, meet many, many, colourful people.

The house itself was a large detached town house, and as we came up the road it loomed over the night, bursting with sound and light, like something out of an Andy Warhol film.

The fence that marked the boundary with the road was the first sign that the night would be one to remember, the wooden slats that made it up had been rearranged to spell out the words "Love House".

Next was the draw bridge, yes that's right the draw bridge, well how else were we to cross the moat, which had been dug around the entire circumference of the building.

In the entrance there was a turnstile. Luckily though, no money was required, and one by one we entered.

On my left I noticed a large Victorian staircase, which as it turned out I wouldn't use until I left, and a room that I briefly noticed was full of people drinking, talking, and smiling. I popped my head into the room that was directly to my right, which was covered wall to wall with padding, no doubt to accommodate the revellers who would from time to time fall from the tyres, bicycles, and various ropes that hung down from the high ceiling. There were even some people swinging and falling from these when I looked in.

I moved through the wide crowded hallway till I came to the next room along. As I entered there greeted me, what was to all intents and purposes, a throne room. Dominating this room was a large table surrounded by maybe half a dozen ornate high backed chairs headed by, what can only be described as, a large throne. There was a large window behind this throne, and at the very moment I walked in Dumbo, yes Dumbo the Walt Disney character, flew past, as if outside. It later transpired there was someone with a cine projector in the rear garden projecting films at this window all night. I stood for more than a moment to take in the scene as people milled about, drinking and having fun.

Then I noticed that in the far corner of the room there was a hole in the floor, a hole with a trap door, and an ant like procession of bodies spilled up into the room making it difficult to enter this exciting looking aperture, but in fairly short order an opportunity to descend arose. Feeling a little tentative, I decided first to pop my head down to see what was there. It was, not surprisingly, a room in the basement of the house.

This room, a large one, was filled with people, all dancing. I climbed down a ladder that was attached to the wall and danced my way through the throng. I stayed in this room for a little while to enjoy the music, which was reggae. The room was, as I've already said, quite large and its walls were covered in egg boxes, with two large speakers in both far corners. It seemed as though there was an extra room in the adjoining wall in which was a window, a quite big window, behind which was a DJ playing the reggae music. After a little while dancing, I noticed that behind the DJ was, apparently, another DJ, and in front of him was another big window. This, I decided was worth investigation.

So I made my way out of this room and into yet another hallway, this one was underground. There was, as I had assumed, another large room, again packed with Terpsichore bodies, I decided not to go in, I'd had a bit of a dance already and I was keen to explore more of this wonderful house.

Looking behind me I saw through the revellers an open door leading to the outside of the building, so out I went to find myself in a small sunken yard occupied by the bottom of a fire escape that went up the side of the building. There were people coming and going on this staircase, which seemed almost to have a party of its own going on. It was on my way up these outside stairs that I noticed the bonfire in the garden, close to which was a music stand, on which was music. In front this there was an elderly man in a bow tie and tails playing a violin, variously different people would come and listen to him.

There was one guy though, a skinhead, who watched him for longer. I'd see him there every time I popped out to make my way up to another floor, there were maybe four or five, or possibly a hundred, (I was altered as I've said) at one point I noticed he'd struck up a discussion with the violin player, who it seemed was explaining its execution, and at yet another excursion onto the fire escape, they'd swapped places and the skin head was playing the violin. I ascended, checking out each floor as I went.

There was room after room filled the funsters enjoying the celebrations. There was a strange kind of organisation to it, each of the rooms was dominated by a different youth sub-culture, in one there were black guys with rainbow coloured woolly hats, in yet another skinheads listening to Ska and the like. An additional room had a mainstay of leather jacketed bikery types listening to heavy metal, and so on, there wasn't any exclusion mind you, and everybody mixed happily.

I made my way up the building in awe of this wonderful place. Everyone partying and dancing and chatting, until I arrived at the attic, the very top of the house, which looked as if it had been set aside as a chill out area.

This was where I finished the party, making joints for a young lady with an abundance of Mary Jane and no ability to roll joints. She had nothing to keep her stash in, so I gave her my, by then, empty stash tin to use for hers.

It was a wonderful night and it will live in my memory forever as a treasured experience. I hope I've managed, my dear non-readers, to impart to you some of the feel and maybe a sense of what an unusual and fascinating experience this was. Thank you for your attention. Please return to your soup.

Mystic Syd's Very Specific Horoscope

Aries
Monday this week will see you being visited by larger than life comedian Jo Brand, who will be expecting sexual favours. So stock up on fags, lard, and cream cakes.
Lucky Car: any Ford

Taurus
You will start the week with an average height of three feet, rising by the end of the week to an excess of ten feet. So mind your head on Friday and Saturday. By Sunday your height won't be such an issue.
Lucky Name: Eugene

Gemini
Wednesday will herald the return of Batman. So my advice would be to make sure all the doors and windows are locked and that Cat woman has been informed.
Lucky Joint: Lamb

Cancer
Beware of rock and pop stars hiding under the bed. Be especially vigilant for Oasis and Brian Ferry. Also. Expect a hail of pasta twist to follow you around from Monday afternoon till late Thursday.
Lucky Sex: Hermaphrodite

Leo
Monday expect a visit from pop goddess Kylie Minogue, who will be expecting Party favours. Warning don't lend her your pen.
Lucky Gland: Pituitary

Virgo
This week your virginity will resurface alternate hours Tuesday and Friday. Try not to get confused, as Friday afternoon will see your sex change as well.
Lucky Phylum: Chordata

Libra

Your natural ability to weight up delicate situations will serve you well this week when you find yourself caught in the middle of a row between Showbiz personalities Cher and Robert Deniro. My advice would be to side with the one most likely to sleep with you.
Lucky Embarrassing Problem: Halitosis

Scorpio

Oh my god, if I were you I just wouldn't get out of bed this week at all. Just stay under the covers until the danger passes.
Lucky Pain Killer: Ibuprofen.

Sagittarius

Due to a freak accident of physics all the floors in your home will be turning a florescent shade of pink. This effect will only be counter actable by eating shoes. Go for it
Lucky Veg: Pak Choy

Capricorn

Are you a fish or a goat? Come on make a decision in your life.
Lucky Envelope: Manila

Aquarius

This week will see your life being taken over by game show host and failed comedian Les Dennis. So don't expect Amanda Holden to answer any of your calls.
Lucky Cheese: Cottage with Pineapple.

Pisces

Time to cast aside those feelings of suspicion its true, everyone does hate you, and don't forget to turn off the gas
Lucky Mollusc: Sea Snail

My Beautiful Ninkompoop

Lumpy bumpy thighs and bum;
Now that depends on your point of view,
Curvy soft and beauty full, is about for me the sum.
You represent love and emotion fresh, exciting clean and new.

I dream of lying next to you:
Arms wrapped around you spooned,
Our bodies laying, side by side, too good to be true.
There is a place inside my heart that has, for you bloomed.

Never have we ever met;
And more, I think, never will we,
Still, it seems, caught I've, been, in your lover net,
And a heart that wants, and could but love, is far away from me.

You're in my head, but every day;
And I dream of you by night.
My love from here, is far away,
But I wish for how it might.

Madonina

The sun is shining it's 35 degrees and there's not a cloud in the sky. The scene before me can only be described as one of extreme natural beauty. I'm sitting on a rock watching children play in a small lake about the size of a large family swimming pool, along the course of the river as it runs down through the valley.

Occasionally the odd tiny lizard pops out to make a personal appearance. After performing a little dance, which involves raising its feet like this: left foot right foot, and then right foot left foot, as if in time to the music of the river as it splashes over the rocks, it runs off to find shade and prepare for its next performance.

I'm getting hot now, and that cold fresh water is looking really inviting, I've been in about four times already, over the last couple of hours, but I can feel the need to jump in building up again as the sweat forms on my brow, I may have to continue in a little while, it's hot … Ok, I've eaten, I had some torta verde, which is basically a fine layer of vegetables and rice spread out over a thinly rolled piece of pasta pastry and baked in an oven. It was delicious, I've had a brief cooling dip, and I've urinated on some ants.

This really is a beautiful place, I love it here. It's like something out of a Bounty chocolate bar advert. Water babbles over the rocks and cascades down a small waterfall into the pool.

This place is called Madonina I have to admit to not being one hundred percent sure of the spelling, but it's certainly close enough, I don't know why it's called that, no one's ever been able to tell me I've asked friends in the past, and they just shrug their shoulders, I do know it's been called this for a very long time. Another thing I know is that when I am here I can actually feel my heart slowing down and I am more relaxed than I would have thought possible.

When I'm in the village I spend more time in this spot, than almost anywhere else. This year, my visit is different, because for the first time I am accompanied by Young Master Charlie Big

Potatoes, he loves it here. With little more than the words ciao and grazie at his disposal, he mixes with the local Bogarts with consummate ease, and he's barely out of the water.

It's crossed my mind that I shouldn't even bother to try and describe this place, because it almost defies description, unless you have knowledge of a similar space in your experience. I can't imagine how it would feel not to have experienced something like it.

I mean it's not like it's that special really, there are, no doubt, many places around the world that have their own versions of Madonnina. Why even in your own land of Albion where the realm is mountainous they surely can be found, admittedly the weather is not as warm, but unquestionably it would be as easy on the eye.

I have in fact, myself, been to similar places in the Land of the Picts in the far North.

If I could, my dear non-readers I'd bring you all here to see it for yourselves, but I can't , so I won't, instead you will all just have to use your imaginations. Ok, I can feel the heat rising and the sweat building, which means it's nearly time for another dip, an appropriate time to bring this piece to a close I feel. So it's into the water once again for me, goodbye and be good to each other. Please return to your soup.

Death by Stan Lee

Normally I'd say I like living in Brighton. It's a great town, full of cultural diversity. You can walk down West Street and catch snippets of conversations spoken by voices from all over the world. There's something for everyone. In the summer the streets are filled with beautiful people, all tanned and healthy looking. Musicians play jazzy tunes to the people sat outside the bars by the beach.

It's also one of the few seaside towns that doesn't die in the winter. Its young and transient nature keeps a vibe going all year round. Still it does quiet down a little in the colder months. Just like anywhere else in the world the cold and dark bring a feeling of gloominess.

I don't like the winter much, I'm a hot weather kind of a guy. I like to be warm. So as I say, normally I like living in Brighton, but this particular cold and wet October morning I would have rather been almost anywhere else.

My name is D. C. I. Peter Norton and I hate rain. It was raining and I was cold and, as if that wasn't bad enough, it was two in the morning and I should have been tucked up in bed. I'd been harshly dragged from under my soft warm duvet to look at a rotting corpse nailed to the side of a wall dressed in a Spider-Man™ outfit.

By the time I arrived the area had already been cordoned off and the investigation was well under way. Pausing briefly to show my identification to a uniform, I wandered over to the heart of the scene, an area taped off in front of a wall.

Nailed to the wall by his wrists and ankles was a Spider-Man™. Later the coroner told me that he'd died the same way you would if you were crucified. As you hang there your own weight crushes your lungs causing asphyxiation, a slow and painful death. He'd been gagged as well, which didn't help.

I watched as two firemen pulled the limp cadaver from the wall. They handled it like it was a rag doll, I remember being surprised it hadn't fallen off the wall already, it was so rotten it must have been up there for some time.

"Chief,"

21

Tommy, my trusty lieutenant, ran over from where he had been interviewing some witnesses, his face hooded under a great big police issue parker.

"So what's this all about?"

I said, looking over at the body as the two firemen laid it on a stretcher, its head lolling to one-side, giant white eyes, staring out from behind black webbing.

"Spider-Man™ Chief."

"Really!"

I said sarcastically.

"Who have we got for suspects then, Dr Octopus™ or maybe the Green Goblin™?"

I shouldn't have snapped but I'd been up for a while now without any coffee. Tommy ignored my mood and carried on.

"The victim has been gagged and nailed to the wall sir, judging by the state of the body, for quite some time. We'll know more after the coroner has had a look."

I'd been a Detective Chief Inspector in Brighton now for three years, seven years as a D. I. and a beat bobby before that, and this was without doubt the most bizarre case I'd ever been involved in.

This was the fifth body we had found and we had no real clues as to the identity of the killer, except that he was probably a fan of comics.

Each murder had been perpetrated as if in homage to a different Marvel comics superhero. The first had been a thirty-two year old barman by the name of James Nash. His body had been found in an abandoned warehouse on an industrial estate in Portslade. The body was so badly burnt he had to be identified by his dental records. He'd been drugged unconscious with a tranquilliser, Benzodiazepine, dressed in a Fantastic Four™ outfit, sort of a blue jumpsuit with a big black number four on the chest, tied to a chair, allowed to wake up, doused in petrol and set alight with a match a la the Human Torch ™.

Two months later we found victim number two, a middle-aged bank manager, Trevor Wilson. He'd been left for dead in the basement of an empty terraced house in Kemp Town. This one had again been drugged and dressed in the colours of the Fantastic Four™, Mr. Fantastic™ this time, the leader of the group, endowed with the ability to stretch his body to fantastic

22

proportions. Trevor had been tied to a homemade rack, again allowed to wake up, and stretched literally until his arms and legs had been ripped from the sockets. He actually died of a heart attack brought on by the shock of the situation.

Ingenious device that rack. It was made out of an old lawn mower engine and some bicycle chains.

We waited another three weeks for our next corpse. He was a gay body builder from Hove. He worked in an office during the week and on evenings and at the weekend he worked on his body. Simon Smith, again drugged, tied hand and foot to a bench press in his own bedroom. His skin had been removed roughly and replaced with flat chunks of brick and stone held together with cement. The whole thing had been painted orange. Wearing only a pair of blue trunks this was yet another member of the Fantastic Four™, The Thing™. Simon had choked to death on his gag when he woke up to find himself skinned alive and covered in bricks, very nasty.

Another month passed before we found the fourth body, a prostitute this time. She'd probably put the costume on herself and willingly, it's not unusual for prostitutes to act out the fantasies of their clients. Jenny Pain was her name. A young blonde girl. Beautiful, only twenty-two, the youngest victim to date.

This time he'd gone for the hands-on approach and strangled her before setting up his scenario. It had all gone on in her own flat; she worked from home, so to speak. After he killed her he went down to the shops and bought gallons of bleach, filled up her bath and left her in it in a vain attempt to emulate the Invisible Girl™, the fourth and final member of the Fantastic Four™.

It was a week later that we found Spider-Man™ nailed up in his grotesque face forward crucifixion. I watched, as the covered body was stretchered into a waiting ambulance. I stuck around for a while checking out some of the evidence, watched the clean-up crew get started, then headed over to the station.

I found Tommy back in the incident room going over the evidence so far.

"So what do we know for sure?"
I pondered openly as I walked over to the incident board.

"Well chief, there's no apparent pattern to the location of the murders. The victims have no connections to each other. The

23

only thing we know for sure is that whoever killed them likes to read comics."

Tommy was right, after months of interviewing witnesses and family members, as well as going over the crime scenes with a fine toothed comb, we knew little more than we did at the start of the investigation. We had one hope of some progress, if there was something with regards to the superhero characters we'd missed. To that end we'd decided to enlist the aid of an expert on the subject.

I knocked on the door of an ordinary terraced house. After a few seconds I heard a chain go across the door and a bespectacled face appeared in the gap between the door and the door frame.

"Hello, Mr. Gawford?" I said to the slightly worried face before me.

"Yes, that's me, can I help you?"
I held my warrant card up to the gap.

"My name is Detective Chief Inspector Norton, and this is my colleague, Detective Inspector Reynolds."

I moved to one side slightly so he could see Tommy behind me.
"We phoned you yesterday regarding an investigation we're conducting at the moment; you may have seen something about it in the paper, the super hero murderer?"
"Oh yes."

The door opened fully to reveal a short, bald, slightly overweight man in his mid to late thirties wearing a well worn t-shirt with, what appeared to me to be, three diagonal rips printed on the front.
"You'd better come in," he said, stepping to one side and motioning for us to enter.

We followed him through the narrow hallway, into a cluttered living area. Piles of graphic novels and comics stood about the room giving the impression of a very scruffy library. A computer stood on an old desk in the far corner, and what looked like large pages of comics lined the walls. I gestured towards them.

Original art work?"

I said trying to give the impression I knew what I was talking about. Mr. Gawford glanced over in the direction of the page I was pointing at.

"Yes, I used to run a comic shop, so I've gotten to know a few artists in my time, I mostly work over the internet now, sell more toys than comics these days mind."

"Yes, that's how we found you, from your site, Premiere Comics.com."

I'd had Tommy spend a couple of hours searching the internet, looking for anyone who might be able to help.
"That's how we got hold of your number."

"I see," he said as he moved a pile of comics, freshly sealed in little comic shaped plastic bags, from an armchair.

"Please sit down."
I took the chair, got out my pad, and glanced at my notes.

"Thanks, now Mister Gawford, as you may know from the newspaper reports, so far we're yet to make any kind of connection between the victims and the, shall we say, methods the murder is using, and what with your knowledge of the subject we thought you might be able to help."

"Right, it's the Fantastic Four™ isn't it?"
He asked.

"Yes that's right, so far,"
I decided not to tell him about finding the last victim, Spider-man™, this morning, until I knew he was going to be able to help, and also we hadn't gone public with it yet.

"How is it, you think, I can help?"
He inquired, settling himself on the chair in front of the computer.

"Well any insight into the circumstances of the characters involved would be useful really as we've mostly drawn a blank so far."
I said.

"Obviously I'll do anything I can to help, although I'm not sure what though?"
He replied.

"What we'd need would be for you to come in to the station and just go over the evidence we have so far, we need an expert on the subject to see if there's any kind of connection between the characters we've missed, anything would be helpful."
He picked up a battered old diary from his desk and started to leaf through it.

"Well I'm pretty busy at the moment. Perhaps I could pop in one afternoon early next week, say Tuesday around two?"
I made a note in my pad, to this effect,
"That would be fine, Mr. Gawford. We'll send a car around at one forty-five to pick you up."
I said.
"Ok then, I'll get together any material regarding the characters I think might be relevant in the mean time, and I'll see you then."
He said as he stood up to see us out.
"Thank you Mr. Gawford. Till Tuesday then."
I took one last glance around the room as we left, taking in a figurine of Spider-Man™ sitting on a shelf as we made our way out. It was in virtually the same pose as our latest victim, which made a tingly shiver run down my spine and the hairs on the back of my neck bristled slightly.

The cold clinical white walls of the autopsy room gave the place an eerie glow that always made me feel a little sick, it's one of those places I never feel comfortable in. The body, now stripped of its costume and partially covered by a starched white sheet, lay on the a table underneath the large surgical lights, which warmed only very slightly the coldness of the room. I stood a little way from the table and coughed to get the attention of the coroner, she looked up from her work and smiled, beckoning me over with a wave.
Honey Delaney, beautiful, blonde, cute, glamorous, all adjectives that describe her perfectly, a woman, who although in her early forties, could quite easily have held her own in a beauty contest with any woman half her age. I'll be honest, I fancied her to bits, she wouldn't have looked out of place in the pages of a nineteen-fifties glamour magazine, she had style. I walked over to her, returning her smile, as I pondered the stark contrast between her good looks and the chill functionality of her surroundings.
"So what have we got?"
I said.
"Well, he's a white male in his mid to late thirties, relatively healthy."
Using her scalpel she pointed to the marks that started at the edges of his mouth and stretched over his cheeks.
"You can see here where the gag was tied around his head, "

26

She moved down his body as she went on,

"and if you look here around the tops of his arms, these marks show how his skin was stretched as his body hung from the wall."

She picked up his arm to show me his wrist,

"And here you can see where the murderer used two nails, one through the palm to hold the hand flat against the wall and another through the wrist to keep the body from falling."

She went on.

"These stretches around the lacerations on his wrists show some signs of struggling, demonstrating that although he was drugged and probably unconscious when he was placed, he almost certainly woke up enough to try and pull himself away before he died."

She paused briefly, and sighed as she said,

"It must have been utterly terrifying."

Honey looked up at me, eye to eye.

"Pete, you have to catch this maniac, no one should have to die like this."

I put my hand on her shoulder,

"We'll do our best Honey I promise".

She wilted a little as if the sadness of this poor man's fate troubled her, and put her scalpel down beside the body. She walked over to a steel table by the wall where she kept a filter coffee machine. She held up a jug of hot coffee, offering me a cup. Never one to refuse a coffee I nodded my head and accepted the offered cup of dark warm liquid, thanking her as I did so.

"Have you worked out when he died yet?"

I asked.

"Well, it's hard to be sure, but judging by the state of decay, I'd have to say the body must have been on the wall for some months, at least three or four, which puts his death at about the same time as the first victim we found, the guy who was burnt alive,"

She picked up her case notes to look up his name,
"James Nash."

I thought for a moment, my investigative instincts started to turn in my mind like the cogs of a clock working around to make the hour hand move, that time of death would mean this fellow was possibly the first victim and not Nash, as we had originally thought.

She took a sip from her coffee,

27

"Any luck identifying him?"
She asked looking over at the slowly decomposing corpse on the table.
I shook my head,
"No, not yet, but we're still waiting to hear from missing persons to see if anyone fits his description. Tommy's over there now, with any luck it won't be too long before we get a positive I.D, but you can never tell with these cases."
Honey nodded knowingly before taking my hand and kissing me gently on my cheek. I had that tingling sensation on my neck again, but this time it was pleasure.

Despite my confident assurances to Honey that it wouldn't take long before we'd find out who Spider-Man™ was, his secret identity if you like, it was actually a few days before missing persons came up with an idea, and it was Monday morning by the time we'd managed to get a relative in to give us a positive I.D. His mother had come in to make the identification. His name was William Spencer, a telesales agent aged thirty-five who still lived with his parents in Beaconsfield Villas.
Tommy and I took his weeping mother, Alice Spencer, home in a squad car. We arrived at the house to find William's younger brother Simon waiting for us at the door. We entered in a line and made our way through to the kitchen where Simon set about making his distraught mother and us a cup of tea. I stood by the door with Tommy in his customary position just behind me. Simon offered us both a chair, and we all sat down and had tea and biscuits while Mrs Spencer collected herself.
"He was a good boy, my Billy,"
She looked up at her remaining son who put his hand on her shoulder,
"We all thought he'd probably gone off on one of his jaunts, he was always going off here and there, he's got friends all over you see,"
She paused briefly as she was overcome by a fit of tears.
"We'd usually get a call from him after a few days, to let us know he was safe and with friends, he was always losing jobs, he had his head in the clouds you see. He was very talented you know Mr Norton, he used to sit where you are now, drawing his pictures, that one was his."
She pointed to a picture blue-tacked to one of the cupboard doors.
I looked up, following her finger, to see a quite competent

rendering of; yes you guessed it, Spider-Man™. The picture had the web-suited hero in an action pose clinging to the side of a building. The pose was reminiscent of Billy's own deathly stance, but there was something else, I'd seen that image before. Then it struck me I looked over at Tommy who was staring at the painting, mouth agape, his head turned slowly to meet my gaze, and I realised that my mouth too was open. I quickly gathered my thoughts and asked to see William's bedroom. The grieving matriarch just nodded and motioned for Simon to show us the way.

His room was small, untidy and crammed full of books and comics, there was hardly any room for Tommy and me to move. The walls were covered in pictures, some was obviously original artwork. I'd learnt enough about the subject lately to recognise that at least.

It was more like the bedroom of a teenager than that of a man in his thirties, there were at least three games consoles crammed into an upturned crate which held atop it, precariously aided by four quite substantial piles of books, a wide screen TV, the likes of which I'd never seen before. The screen was as big as a bus, and from the side it was a thin as a wafer, honestly if you'd run into the room without knowing it was there, it would have cut you in half, right down the middle.

Comics and assorted action figures were ranged around the room, some on shelves, and the far wall was stacked high with boxes jammed full of comics, graphic novels, and all manner of comic memorabilia. I bet if I was to ask you for a theme, no, better yet, a colour scheme, I'd put a month's pay on you saying red and blue, because, if one thing was clear, it was that Billy was a fan of Spider-Man™.

He was everywhere, there was even an ancient looking life size, well almost, jointed cardboard cut-out of the web headed vigilante pinned to his ceiling. It was the closest thing we'd had to a break from the beginning of this investigation, a proper link between the victim and his character.

I picked up a pile of photos from a shelf and started to flick through them. As I did something caught my eye, and I stopped at a picture of three teenagers at a comic convention wearing fairly, although homemade looking, respectable replicas of super-hero costumes. I immediately spotted Mr Spencer in the middle of the trio, smiling thumbs-up to the camera with his mask in his hand; obviously, the one in a Spider-Man™ outfit, to his right, was a

29

handsome young chap with bleached blonde hair, in a Fantastic Four™ costume. I was pretty good at spotting those by then. There was something familiar about him, but I couldn't quite put my finger on it.

To William's left, with one arm around his shoulder, the other raised aloft in a cheer, fully masked up in a bright yellow jumpsuit with black tiger stripes on the torso, which I would later learn was a Wolverine™ costume, was the shortest of the group, and there was something about his smile, I recognised it.

"Hey, is that a very young Nash?"
It was Tommy over my shoulder. He was pointing to the photo, at the figure to the right of William Spencer to be precise.

"And he's dressed like the Human Torch™, wasn't that his character?"
I looked and looked again, and then I saw it. It was Nash; he must have been no more than seventeen or nineteen tops. My heart stopped for a moment, this was it. The break we'd been waiting for. A link, a proper link, Nash and Spencer had been friends. Nash had been a problem for us from the start. He'd had no living relatives and his flat; a sparse and minimally decorated place, had given us little in the way of clues, in the end we'd managed to identify him through a dental records search.

I looked up at Tommy, his eyes turned to me and his shocked and puzzled expression started to change, as the light of realisation dawned, to a smile. In a moment we were both back downstairs at the kitchen table with Mrs Spencer and Simon.

"James Nash?"
She pondered briefly,

"Oh yes, James, I remember him. Billy and James were good friends," she paused, "but Billy can't have seen James for, oh, it must be fifteen years or more now."
I paused briefly from my note taking.

"Do you remember why Billy hadn't seen James for so long, Mrs Spencer, did they fall out?"
She took a kitchen towel from a roll on the table and mopped her eyes, already very puffed up and red from crying. She took a deep breath, and looked at the picture again.

"They were friends from school. It was the shop, I think? Yes, they all fell out over the shop. I don't remember that much about it really, it was all quite a while ago."

She stopped, as once more she realised her son was dead, and burst into tears.

Simon knelt and put his arm around his mother protectively and looked at me accusingly.

"Do you have to do this now; can't you see she's in no condition to deal with all your questions at the moment?"

The grieving mother, with obvious effort, pulled herself together and patted her surviving son's arm.

"It's ok Simon."

She turned to me, struggling to contain herself, clearly drawing on what emotional reserves she had left. "Inspector, do you think there's some connection between Billy's death and James?"

Then it occurred to me that if the Spencers hadn't had any contact with Nash for so many years then they may not know of his death.

"Yes I do Mrs Spencer, James Nash was the first victim we found, please, anything you can tell me about James and William's relationship may well help?"

A look of shock came over her face.

"My God, James is dead as well?"

She once more returned her gaze to the photo of the three erstwhile superheroes, and regarded it silently for a moment.

"Years ago James and Billy opened a comic shop together, I think it was called First Comics? Anyway, it was in the lanes, for the first year or so it was all ok, they made money. Then something went wrong. What was it now?"

She paused and considered the photo again.

"Oh I remember, there was some kind of dispute with their other friend, this is him."

She said pointing to the third member of the trio in the picture.

"What was his name, Gary was it? I can't remember. I do remember that James and Billy fell out with him first, and then it was six months after that the shop closed, and that was when Billy and James fell out."

Her eyes started to mist over as she realised she was never going to see her son again. She started to sob, gently at first, then more vigorously, after a few weepy minutes she was able to manage her grief once more.

"I'm so sorry gentlemen, what must you think of me, I must look a right state."

I put my hand gently on her arm.

"It's quite all right Mrs Spencer, we understand, this must be very hard for you, we'll leave you now, but I may have some

31

more questions for you in the next few days, thank you, you've already been a great help, and I promise you,"
I took her hand in mine,
"we will catch the man who took your son from you. Thank you again, we'll see ourselves out."

I spent the drive back to the station barking, orders at Tommy.
"Right, Tomorrow I'm going to go over all of the case files from all of the victims so far. I want to be completely sure that they have no links what so ever to their super hero, it can't be a coincidence that Spencer and Nash were in those particular costumes, also we'll need to find out as much as we can about their shop First Comics, and we need to find out who was in that Wolverine™ costume."
I looked across at Tommy who was driving.
"I feel this case breaking Tommy; we're close, so very close."

The next day I spent most of the morning going over the evidence we had on the rest of the victims in the incident room, while Tommy was out trying to gather information about Nash and Spencer's shop. I was looking for links between them and their characters, but neither the prostitute Jenny Pain, the bank manager Trevor Wilson, nor the body builder Simon Smith, had any apparent links to their respective hero's or, in fact comics at all. The only link was still that they all made up the rest of the Fantastic Four™. What was I missing, there had to be a reason that they had been chosen, how could Nash and Spencer, who we now knew where the first two victims, be so closely linked and yet the other three not? It didn't make sense, unless, and this was the idea that I had kept coming back to me all morning, they, Nash and Spencer, had been killed for a specific reason, revenge for example, and then the killer had gotten a taste for it and decided to carry on randomly killing?

I was at my wits end; I picked up the photo of Nash, Spencer and Wolverine™, trying to will it to solve the case for me. I had that feeling I get, like a sixth sense, that the investigation was coming to an end, it was on the tip of my tongue, but there was something I was missing, something staring me in the face. Try as I might I couldn't place it. Then there was a knock at the door.

"Come,"

I said distractedly, still considering the photo from Spencer's room. The desk Sergeant poked his head around the door.

"A Mr Gawford to see you, sir,"

He said. Then I remembered that earlier I'd sent a car to pick up our comics expert.

"Oh yes, send him in, please Sergeant,"

I said, idly dropping the photo onto the desk.

The door opened all the way and in walked the bespectacled, permanently slightly nervous figure of Larry Gawford.

He had quite a heavy looking rucksack over one shoulder, and walked towards me, hand extended in greeting. I took it, noticing as we shook how sweaty it was.

"Please, Mr Gawford, have a seat."

As he sat he placed his bag on the table and started to unload a number of comics and papers onto the desk.

"I wasn't really sure what I should bring, so I just piled a load of stuff into a bag, I hope it helps?"

He said enquiringly.

I sat down opposite him to look over his pile of comics,

"Frankly Mr Gawford any insight into the case you can give would be of help."

I picked up a comic that had slid from the pile as Mr. Gawford had been piling them up. It was a copy of Marvel Team Up™, specifically number two, from May 1972, featuring Spider-Man™ and the Human Torch™. It occurred to me that it was a strangely pristine object for something so old and I wondered, for a moment, how long it had been inside its plastic comic shaped bag. What was I missing; it was here I was sure it was.

I spent the next hour or so with Larry, as he insisted I call him, going over the history of the fantastic four. As it turned out there was quite a lot of history between the characters of the Fantastic Four™ and Spider-Man™. For example in one of his earliest adventures Spider-Man™ had tried and failed to get them to let him join, Gawford even had a copy of a comic called "What if" which told the story of what might have happened if Peter Parker™ had of become a member of the team and they'd changed their name to the Fantastic Five™. The main feeling I got from it all was that there was a definite link between the super hero team and Spider-Man™, particularly Spider-Man™ and the Human Torch™, who it seems had often been portrayed as close friends. Although it hadn't really answered the questions I'd hoped it would, it had definitely given me some things to think about, and proved that there was more than a coincidental link between the costumes and the victims, certainly in the case of Nash and Spencer.

Mr Gawford started to pack his stuff away, barring a couple of comics I'd asked him if I could keep in the hope they might lead to some inspiration, as I called through to the desk sergeant to escort him out of the station. He was picking up a couple of the comics, from the now cluttered desk, when the photo of Nash, Spencer and Wolverine™ fell to the floor, it had become slightly stuck to the bottom of one of the comics. Gawford paused briefly upon seeing the photo, as I bent to pick it up, I noticed him flinch for a second as he noticed the scene of the three chums, and he seemed in rather more of a hurry to leave than he had been a moment ago, but before I could give it any real thought the desk sergeant arrived and Larry quickly left the room, smiling and hurriedly saying goodbye.

I was still sat looking at the photo when Tommy burst into the room brandishing a small wad of documents from Company's House. Eyes wide and full of excitement he placed the papers in front of me triumphantly.
"Look you'll never believe it!" He said.
I picked up the pages and leafed through them searching for the source of his excitement. Then I saw it, the name of the third partner in the business. It was Gawford, the man who just a short time before had been sat in the very same chair that Tommy was now.

It was less than half an hour before we found ourselves once again at the door of an ordinary terraced house, only this time the door was slightly ajar, as if whoever had opened it had arrived in a hurry. Tommy entered first ,calling out,
"Mr Gawford, it's Detective Inspector Reynolds and Detective Chief Inspector Norton, we wondered if we could clear up a couple of things with you."
There was no reply.
I followed Tommy into the building as he continued to call out his name into the deathly quiet hall.
The door to the front room was shut. Tommy twisted the handle and peered inside, I heard a sharp gasp leave his lips. As

he stopped dead he let go of the handle and the door swung slowly all the way open. I looked around Tommy to see what had made him gasp. Then as I saw it I felt the shock hit me like a sledge hammer, there swinging slightly from a rope attached to an exposed beam in the ceiling, squeezed into his now old worn and ill-fitting Wolverine™, costume was Larry Gawford.

I found a hastily scribbled note on the floor by the upturned chair that he had used to stand on before kicking it way. It told how over the years the bitterness and hate had festered inside, eating at his soul; until he'd been driven to exact revenge on the two men he believed had ruined his life.

The act of committing the first two murders had driven him to a kind of obsessive compulsive madness that lead him to a sort of crazy desire to complete his work. He'd felt he had to find away to add the rest of the Fantastic Four™, eventually getting a taste for the killing. There was a file box on the desk that contained photos of all of the victims along with detailed logs of their comings and goings, as well as an A4 sheet of paper divided down the middle with a brief list of regular names on one side and a list of super hero names on the other, the first three names Jenny Pain, Trevor Wilson, Simon Smith, were crossed out, leaving only five. When I saw this the first thought that went through my head was that at least we saved the Hulk™.

The End.

Happy

It's really just a feeling,
So simply you can say,
It often leaves you reeling,
And sometimes goes away.

It's right to sometimes leave you,
It is the case you see,
For true appreciation,
It's absence is the key.

Smiling isn't difficult,
Unless it's all the time,
then it can be tiresome,
For which I have no rhyme?

Sadness isn't happy,
But it's important too,
How would you know you're happy,
If sadness, you never knew?

So remember to be sad at times,
It's your feelings you must free,
Sadness brings you balance,
So happy you can be.

Friendship

There are some people in the world we consider using the word "friends", but what does that really mean?
What is a friend? My mother has always maintained that if you can count the people you consider to really be your friends on one hand, then you are doing well.

There are those people, those constants, people who persist, people who you don't have the commitment of family with, but who nevertheless continue regularly be to people who appear throughout our lives, the frequent players in the acts of our existence.

All of the people we call friend must by definition be people to whom we were attracted, for something or other about them that was interesting, a hat, a performance, or a way of standing, a particular flattery they paid us, it could have been anything.

Some people whisk you up in a whirlwind of flattery and compliments and you dance and sing, and then they get bored and drop you just as quickly, and sometimes we do that as well, and that's fine, even wonderful, as well as valid. Sometimes those whirlwind friendships will find a level at which they can be sustained and that is even finer, more wonderful and the ultimate in the validation of your personal worth. But the people who are really worth your time and your energy are the people who will forgive you, if you get it wrong from time to time, the people who aren't going the change their mind at the drop of hat or a misjudged emotional reaction.

If people mean what they say, and follow up with sincerity and an emotional commitment that endures, then you know they "care" about you and how you feel, and they are worth it.

I see a number of my non-readership baulking there at the word commitment. This is not to be mistaken for singularity of affection and is not limited finitely. It is I suppose simply the difference between being utterly fickle, by dropping people you made definite emotional overtures to, and not being so, by not dropping them. It's just, I guess, about meaning what you say. It's about responding to a good morning and remembering how you promised this and that and then coming through on those promises in one way or another. And again that's not an exclusive thing. On the contrary, it's an all inclusive thing we all have that responsibility and we should, if we're emotionally mature enough, be able to achieve it.

I believe I do have those friends, the ones that are numerically ascendant on the digits of one hand. They are old friends and they are new ones. One I've not even met but know that they will be an "Iceboxes" friend forever, and yet another is a right bleeding misery, sometimes, that I love and care for deeply and I couldn't get rid of if I tried.

I do love to make friends and meet people and laugh and sing and dance and experience the lives of others and I will, I know, as my life so far has shown me, continue to "make" friends. And the key I think is being happy with yourself and part of being happy with yourself is acknowledging that sometimes we get it wrong, and if someone loves you, I mean really loves you properly freely and without condition, then they'll be there to say, "Hey, no don't,"

Or they'll say "You hurt, I'm sorry,"

And maybe even "Remember, I love you,"

They won't just flit away at the first sign that you have a flaw, like a flighty, if beautiful, butterfly that has used up all the nectar of the flower that it has flattered so. This they feel as something like sympathy, not to be mistaken for pity. Friendship is caring for another being. It's making soup for, or taking DVD's round to occupy a sick friend, it's about helping and being there, in the ways you can, it's not forced or hard or a chore, it's about wanting to make the effort and that effort coming easily and naturally.

Please return to your soup.

38

Cosa hai fatto Oggi? (August 2009)

I'm sitting in a bar in a medieval village in the foothills of the Alps, what they call the Maritime Alps. A man is sitting to my right, he's my cousin. His name is none of your concern. It suffices to say he's known to me.

I've known him since I was a young boy and he was a young man, he's Italian. He's used a lot of drugs in his life. In the beginning they were recreational, as I understand it, mostly cocaine and heroin. I'm not surprised such things are easy to come by in this part of the world. It's come to be known as "La Costa Dell' Eroina".

A little usage became a habit, which in turn became dependence so, to help him with his addiction it was decided he should be given more drugs, prescribed medications this time. The same virtually as the ones he'd been taking recreationally. Only more refined, stronger versions, so he wouldn't need quite as much and then, using the new drugs, he could be weaned off the recreational ones. He still uses these prescribed medications today, years later.

He looks much older than he is. He can only be in maybe his fifties? Though he looks like a man of sixty perhaps even seventy.
He's bought me a coffee, and we sit pretty much in silence. I've got a book it's called, "The Mechanism" by John T Sladek, I'm not reading it, I'm mostly watching him. Occasionally he looks up at me and I'll smile at him.

I always give him my biggest broadest smile and sometimes a wink. To which he'll usually give me a little smile back. I ask him what he's been doing today, "Cosa hai fatto oggi?"

He tells me he's been watching the television. I ask him what he was watching, but he doesn't remember so he returns to

39

what's occupied him for most of the time we've been sitting with each other.

He's got a ritual, he repeats the same actions over and over again. I've been watching for a while now, and I think I've got it. I get my note-book out and start to write down exactly what he does:

He rolls a cigarette, he lights it. He rests his head in his left hand with his elbow resting on the table. He focuses his eyes on the ashtray. He takes a couple of puffs on his cigarette then the ritual starts in earnest. He dabs his fag (cigarettes are often called that in England) on the bottom of the ashtray, then he brings it to his lips. He licks his lips, puffs and again licks his lips, repeating the process several times. Then he takes a couple of puffs, unnecessarily re-lighting his smoke as he does so.

Once pointlessly re-lit the process starts, all over again, until the rollie (a British colloquialism for a hand rolled cigarette) is finished and he starts afresh with a new paper...

A Rose Without It's Thorns

A Galleon, without cannons
Snakes, without venoms
A Lion, without claws
An Eagle, with talons
Bulls, without horns
A Rose, without its thorns

The Pointlessness, of empty threats
The Insult of, indifferent hearts
And Boredom, with some irksome parts
Unendingly, Tiresome talk of tripe
Of Lackluster, rear end swipes
A Rose, without its thorns

Of Burnt out dreams, and awkward ends
With Wasted things, and spirits bent
And Tired youth, a waste of time
Never To have know your touch
A Life without the scent of you
A Rose without its thorns

Ego

People talk a lot about ego. What is it though and what does it mean to the way we see ourselves? Jung's Ego wasn't the thing it is today, more latterly it seems that ego is a byword to describe someone who you believe thinks they are better than you, This is a more modern view of ego and is about personal perception, and

the perceptions others have of us, let's look at that. There is, it seems to me, a fragile balance to be struck between knowing yourself and your place in the Universe and acknowledging the sensibilities of others. We can't take responsibility for someone else's feelings, but we can be understanding, and I think it's important to help, when we can, other people find ways to love themselves, and understand that they have to know and love themselves before anyone else will.

So it's ok to have an ego, to feel good about yourself it's fine, trust me you can like you, it's ok and it's not wrong. The only people who will think this is wrong are the particularly pious and those who think that feeling good about themselves involves making you feel bad. I think the key is a healthy balanced idea of yourself and the world you live in, your world.

Having an ego isn't the problem, it really is ok, even desirable, to think highly of yourself, the problems only start when you take it all seriously. I can't stress that bit enough, stop for a minute and think, "Yes I think I'm great, but how seriously do I take that?"

Let's look at it in a graphic way, using a number of over complicated and unnecessary metaphors. I see the ego as an enormous construct made of concrete stone and steel, a healthy one is big and strong, and it gets built up over time as we make ourselves better people by helping and smiling a lot, and it can get huge, but that's ok, like I've already said it doesn't matter how big it gets, it's as big as you feel good about yourself, its size really is unimportant in relation to itself. It's the height of the legs that matter, and the legs, in stark contrast to the ego, the legs that hold it up are fragile.

42

They are thin and made of glass, they are representative of how important you think you are. The more important you believe yourself to be the longer the legs will get, pushing the ego higher and higher away from the ground, and as they get higher they get weaker.

This is where the danger is, egos are fine just as long as you keep them just off the ground, there's more you see, not only does the ego have legs to keep it off the ground, it also has an elastic like substance that is attached to both it and the ground directly underneath it. This is called "the sense of humour" and as the legs grow the "the sense of humour" is stretched, and it can take some stretching, I can tell you.

The more it stretches the less effective it becomes, it gets less and less able to understand "jokes" and makes us laugh, not when we think a joke is funny, but when we see other people laughing, consequently we do it so as not to look stupid, hence the phrase, "He who laughs last… didn't get the joke in the first place," but this stretching has an effect on the legs and they will weaken still further as "the sense of humour" is stretched to glass leg breaking point.

Even at this time, the situation is still retrievable and if you are concerned that you may be taking yourself too seriously, sit down and watch two Marx Brothers films in a row. If you don't do this you are in danger of an "ego collapse". There is, even at this advanced stage, one or two early warning signs.

Tiny cracks will start to appear in one or more legs, and it only takes one, the crack will get bigger and bigger, and as "the sense of humour" starts to say, "why would a chicken cross the road anyway?" a leg will snap, and you only need one to go, (did I mention there were four, no? Well there are four legs,) and the whole ego will come crashing down to the ground. Bang! And the cert is gone. Next, self loathing will set in, or violence, probably even both. You'll feel shit and start to hurt people. So remember don't take it seriously and you'll be ok.

Please return to your soup.

Wow!

I feel my eyes close and suddenly the normal spots of light that inhabit the backs of my eyelids begin to coalesce into a tunnel that stretches a million zillion miles in all directions.

This space is filled with what I can only describe as fractal like patterns, although that is hardly an adequate description (curse the corporeal nature of language). Everything is moving although it doesn't occur to me at the time to wonder if it's me that is moving or if this strange new reality is the source of all of the movement?

Then from out of the patterns, the form of a girl appears, a beautiful girl, she is smiling at me, welcoming me arms out stretched, she giggles a little. I get from her a sense of introduction; as if this is just a taste of things to come, then she merges back into the swirling world of colour and light.

Next from the ether comes an Escher like form of Egyptian women (again there are no real words to describe this vision) they move around each other and around me, filling me with an all over feeling of well-being. Smiling and giggling at me, I feel myself smiling and I giggle. It is at about this point that I wonder what will happen if I opened my eyes. I do (but only for the briefest of moments) and I see my living room. For a fleeting moment the alterations that have occurred in reality shock me, I come close to feeling fear, but it passes quickly.

I believed that I knew what it was to hallucinate. I was wrong, I've never seen anything like this before, with or without my eyes open. The world is an ever changing swirl of purples and blues. Although I can recognize my front room it is not my front room. I can see Marc (the facilitator) smile at me. He giggles and I can see the giggles feel his joy at my condition.

Callum (my friend and observer) rises from the chair and stays in the chair at the same time until there is an endless chain of Callums between the chair and the door all of them as solid as the next. Then I close my eyes again and return to the other dimension, (it's all so real, can it be described as hallucination?). There are more of the same visions although the inhabitants of this world appear to have taken their leave of me. But I know instinctively I will meet them again. After what seems like a life time I open my eyes again look at Marc and say, "Wow!"

Nose who Knows?

A sensual world that governs plight,
Never more than that, who knows?
Hidden? Yes, though in plain sight,
As plainly faced, behind your nose.

Dusty, earthy, wet and sweet.
Liquored veins for gods implore.
When raining hits the dries of peat.
Delight of this named petrichor.

Odiferously we make our way.
Through a reeking world we go.
This is the free olfactory play.
That will lead where, who knows?

Of animals and fur and strife.
Ground abound from dawn til dusk.
The tangy force that tells of life.
The vibrancy best known as musk.

Noses though sometimes will turn.
Away from the fetid stench.
When nauseating, or stale discern.
From our faces these we wrench.

So go abroad, a world to smell.
And learn, as though you might.
Miasma led you will compel.
Is this love we all requite.

Zippy, George and Bungle; The Biographies

Zippy

Having a zip for a mouth might, for some, be thought of as a handicap. Not for Zippy, real name Norman Zipaoski. The only child of post war Polish immigrants, Alexandra and Boris. His was a childhood of hardship and deprivation. Nevertheless, young Norman was headed for the top! His mother had said of him from the day he was born, "That boy has stars in his eyes." After a number of years working as a sheet metal worker by day for a living, and doing the rounds on his local club circuit by night, he had his first big break when, eventually, he had a meeting with the hippo who was to change his life. Known only as George, the hippo's naive styling's wooed audiences around the country. They immediately gelled as a double act and were a hit in all the working men's clubs. It was here they were seen by an up and coming television producer looking for a double act for a new TV show called Rainbow, the rest is history.

George

Life's not easy for pink hippo's…

George's career in the entertainment world has always been an uphill struggle. Fighting prejudice at every corner, George's struggle is an inspiration to us all showing us neither colour nor creed can hold back talent…

George grew up in the Serengeti and it was clear in the early days his unusual colouring was both a gift and a curse. His Mother was a rock in his infancy and nurtured his acting talents throughout childhood, but David Attenborough and the other wildlife film makers didn't seem to want a pink hippo

Undaunted his mum used her showbiz connections to set up George on a tour of the UK's working men's clubs, here a chance meeting with the son of a Polish sheet metal worker would change his life forever.

As a double act George and Zippy wowed the public and agents alike, it wasn't long before the pair were snapped up by light entertainment's giant Rainbow.

Bungle

Nobody could have predicted the strange series of events that would rocket this simple bear to a life of international stardom. Born, like most bears, in the woods of Bratislava, his early years were an idyll of peace and harmony, which for this young bear wasn't nearly exciting enough, leading him to pack his knotted hanky and make for the big city. Arriving in London only fifteen years later, he started his career. dancing to simple tunes, "Baa, Baa Multicultural sheep," "Itsy Bitsy Spider," and "Hickory Dickory Dock," to name but three, as a street performer in London's Covent Garden. While on the streets living out his paw to mouth existence he was spotted, caught in a net, taken straight to the Thames Television studios and released into what was to become his new home. After years as one of the country's top performers Bungle has recently published his autobiography, "The Bear Facts".

People, "Love Pies" and Emotional Ownership

People, it seems, can be very easily confused on a number levels about what 'love is'. There are those, for example, who are content to see it as two naked caricature children wearing fig leaves, which is a slightly limited and shallow view, but hurts no one, so is fine. Others see it as hearts, flowers, cards and chocolates, these are things really only meant as a way of expressing our love, all be it in a tooth decaying style in the case of chocolate, but that aside, this interpretation of love is essentially harmless, and can bring smiles, so it can never hurt to use this method, I mean who doesn't like to get lovely presents? I know I do, although to over subscribe is dangerously close to the naked fig leafed children and therefore shallow.

Then we come to the those who dish their love out as if it were a pie, I've already brought the love pie to your attention, dear non-reader, in an earlier poem, 'The Love Pie'. I fear this expression of love has a set of problems all its own.

People have a tendency to use it to stamp ownership on each other's emotions, they give each other a slice of love pie, "there that's my love portion for you, that you own". They dish it out, in a hierarchy of pie shaped slices in different sizes. The most beloved getting the largest slice, God forbid, though, there's any irregularity, "hang on you just gave a "me" sized slice of pie, with kissing and sauce, to that person, but I gave you my piece of pie that shape, and you used it to touch me?" I imagine it can be quite the most difficult thing to keep up with who you love, when, where and with which slice?

Anger, jealousy, dishonesty, pain, and emotional blackmail, are, it would seem, the main ingredients of the Love Pie. It requires an instant response, "I messaged you with my declaration of love, why haven't you responded to the fifty other e-mails I've sent, there were naked children didn't you see them, they had fig leaves?" They will stand there brandishing their emotional cake slices, insisting that you return their slice in equal

49

measure, the trouble is they, as is the way all metaphorical things, don't really know how much pie they should be getting back, so whatever you give will either seem too little, or so much is returned, they become scared and run away.

The Love Pie can cause parents to reject their children, over new lovers It creates dangerous things like Scientology and other cults, which use a kind of inverted mass Love Pie that saps the love out of people, causing them to reject family members, often the only people who do love us without reserve.

These people, I fear, may be in the majority, but not you of course, my dear non-reader, I've no doubt that you are one of the few of us who love without resort to restriction, I'm sure your love is great enough to make those it is directed towards feel as free as the wind, and able to love who they please, and not confined in Evelyn De Morgan's 'Gilded Cage'.

If you really love someone, especially romantically, you'll love them freely and honestly, because then and only then will they love you back with truth and passion.

Don't try and give it a quotient, or measure that which is returned, and if it's not returned, don't blame others for not feeling as you do, get over it and find the people who do.

Look for love not ownership, and make feeling it a joy, not a chore. Please return to your soup.

No Regret

Fleetingly we came together;
In fun and prose and passion,
Nothing ever lasts forever.
Ended gently in a fashion.

Moved was I, by tender charms;
Your beautifully inspired mind.
The place you rested in my arms,
Future comforts I can find,

Fortunately and well met;
So gleefully we danced and loved,
Nowhere in this I find regret,
Resultant friendship, and found trust.

51

Some Things People have Said to Me

"What are you, crazy?"

"Just fuck off!"

"I'm rowing away from Bergerac."

"You're the Doctor Who Man!"

"I've got my knob out."

"how come you're so stupid?"

"Are you actually really clever?"

"Shit with sugar on."

"I thought you'd like it?"

"I love you."

"I hate you!"

"What you need is a horse."

"It's just self indulgent wank."

"How do you do that?"

"Why did you do that?"

"You're a nice guy."

"You're a bastard!"

"Do you want ace in that?"

"Cum on my picture."

"Mmmm that's good."

"You should open a school."

"You've got great legs."

"That's not your name?"

"I've got forty minutes, are you going to fuck me?"

"Wow, you really were telling the truth!"

"I don't find anyone attractive."

"Oooo, I'm going to take you home."

"You're just a slut."

"You're a funny man."

"Your style reminds me of Rob Newman."

You're not funny."

"Do you see this man in court today?"

"We are called Strawberries are not necessary before the comes."

"You look like Salman Rushtie."

"You look like Rowan Atkinson."

"You look like the guy from Leon."

"You look like Gazza."

"What the fuck is that on your head?"

"Show me your cock."

"You're my renaissance man."

"You're a useless piece of shit."

"I think you have a very old soul."

"My god you were telling the truth!"

"Yeah well Italian and Spanish are the same thing."

"Why do you think I seek out your company?"

"I Know I can tell you anything."

"I'm better looking that you, more intelligent that you, I've got more money that you, why do you get women and I don't?"

"I don't care what anyone says, just as long as I'm always welcome here."

"Did you do that?"

"You ruined her for other men!"

"Us weirdoes have to stick together."

"You can feel the dolphin, what dolphin?"

"Oh, that was good."

"You weren't like that with me?"

"What just because I didn't fancy him?"

"Yes."

"No."

"I don't like you at all, I'm only here because other people seem to and I can meet people that way."

"By the third. you will die."

"You are my friend and I'm glad you are as well!"

Do you mind if I Join you?

1) A chance meeting.

He'd always like this cafe, not least because of its name. It was called the "Dumb Waiter" you see and this he found quite charming. It was a great place to sit and watch the world go by. His usual spot was in the corner by the window. He'd come here often, to while away an afternoon with a coffee and perhaps a bacon sandwich whilst he perused a copy of Private Eye a newspaper or perhaps a book. Sometimes he might chat briefly to a fellow patron at an adjacent table, occasionally even being joined by a friend but mostly he would sit alone and just watch the people as they walked by, going about their business but on this particular sunny summer afternoon, he was to find himself making a new friend.

He'd always had an eye for the girls and now in his mid forties, that hadn't changed so of course he'd noticed her as soon as she'd entered the busy cafe. She was young, perhaps twenty or so years of age. Quite simply, he'd found his eye draw to her as she'd breezed in, fresh as a daisy. She wasn't tall, about five foot four, and in her light summer dress she exuded a youthful beauty that made him smile. After ordering a croissant and a mug of tea she made her way down to the seating area. He was sat at the only table with a space on it, which necessitated that she approach his corner of the cafe so with her newly acquired beverage and pastry she politely enquired of him.

"Do you mind if I join you"?

He looked up at her and smiled, she was a pretty girl, and with no makeup on, she had an easy beauty that was natural and fresh.

"Please do".

He said with a pleasant smile on his face.

Returning his smile and saying thank you, she placed her lunch on the table and sat down opposite him. For a few minutes they sat in silence and he returned his attention to the crossword clue he was puzzling over in an abandoned copy of The Independent, that was on the table when he'd sat down. Reaching into her bag she pulled out a book, he noticed it was "Of Mice and Men" by John Steinbeck, a book he'd read himself, first as a young man and once or twice in the intervening years since. He found his gaze drawn to her every now and then, over the top of the paper as she nibbled her Croissant, sipped her tea and concentrated on her novel. He'd mostly finished the crossword and currently found himself perplexing, a bit, over one particular clue, which caused him to think out loud without realising it, saying.

"Factory worker usually found carding flax, mm"?

"Is it, heckler"?

Looking up from his concentration, it took him a moment or two to realise it was her who had spoken. He'd gotten so involved in thinking about the clue that, for a moment, he'd forgotten she was even there.

" Oh, erm"?

He mumbled, looking back down at the crossword. He had the "h" and the "l" from the answers to a couple of other clues.

"Yes, yes I think it is, thank you. I was starting to think I was never going to get it".

He said, pleased she'd spoken.

"Sorry, I hope I didn't spoil it for you"?

Said she.

"Oh no, that's fine, thank you".

He thought for a moment.

57

"I'm nearly finished, but there's still a few clues left, perhaps you'd like to help me get those as well"?

She smiled, nodded, and putting aside her book she joined him in his hunt for answers and they spent the next twenty minutes or so engaged in finishing the crossword together.

"thank you for letting me help, my name's Lottie by the way".

She told him, offering her hand.

"Hello Lottie, I'm Sid, pleased to meet you".

Said he, taking the offered hand and shaking it warmly.

Not wanting the conversation to stop, and gesturing to her book he said.

"So, have you read any other Steinbeck"?

She picked up the book and thumbed it a little idly, replying.

"Yes I've read Cannery Row, have you read any"?

he confirmed her suspicion that he had indeed read few of the authors other books. One thing led to another, till they found themselves spending the next couple of hours or so, discussing not only literature but as such conversations are often inclined grow, also films as well as music, art and all sorts of things they enjoyed, without really telling each other anything about themselves, until before they knew it they were the only patrons left in the cafe. It was early evening and they noticed the staff had started to discreetly clean up around them.

Sid looked at his watch.

"Goodness look at the time! I'd really better be getting off, I going to meet up with some friends later, but I've really enjoyed chatting with you this afternoon Lottie, I hope we get to do it again sometime, tell you what let's keep an eye open for each other"

She smiled and with a little nod of agreement, they shook hands, and parted company on that, the first day of their acquaintance.

2) Happy happenstance.

The Train wasn't due to leave for another half an hour, so the carriage was mostly empty, Lottie liked it when it was like that simply because, as she had her choice of seating, she could, if she liked, sit at a table. Choosing one about half way up the carriage, she settled down with her coffee and got out her newly acquired kindle, she loved to read, and was really enjoying her new piece of technology, her boyfriend Mark had bought it for her recent birthday, already loaded up with books. The novel she had chosen to start with was one by an author she hadn't come across before, Kurt Vonnegut, it was called "The Player Piano".

It was shaping up nicely, she was less than a chapter in and already engrossed when, as the train started to pull away, a vaguely recognised voice said.

"Do you mind if I join you"?

She looked up from her book, to see the pleasantly cheerful face of Sid looking down at her.

Smilingly and remembering how he had replied on their previous and first meeting she said.

"Please do".

He took the seat opposite her, and placing his latte on the table, settled in for the journey.

"Hello Lottie, fancy seeing you here and how lovely it is to see you again so soon, how are you"?

He said, the pleasure of this marvelously coincidental second meeting apparent on his face.

"I'm good thanks, It's lovely to see you too and you, how are you"?

She replied.

"Yeah I'm fine thanks, I'm so please to bump into you again, I really enjoyed the afternoon we spent chatting in the cafe, the other week, it's not often an old fellow like me gets to chat with a beautiful young lady such as yourself".

She blushed a little at his flattery.

"So, have you got a crossword for us to do then"?

She asked.

"I'm afraid not, I've brought a book with me this time, I find a train journey can go much so more pleasantly with a good story".

He replied, as he reached into his hold all to get out his book, revealing it to be, in what Karl Gustav Jung would have called a synchronicity, "Timequake" also by Kurt Vonnegut. Lottie started to laugh, almost knocking over her paper cup in her amusement.

"What on earth are you laughing at girl, are you OK"?

said Sid, slightly taken aback by this strange outburst of mirth.

Still giggling Lottie showed him the front of her Kindle, revealing the cover of her own Vonnegut novel. after a bit of a double take Sid couldn't help but have a little chortle himself at this strange coincidence.

"Well how about that"?

He said.

"I know".

Replied Lottie, going on.

"What a bizarre coincidence! Have you read many of his book then"?

She asked.

"Oh, yes, most of them I think, interestingly enough The Player Piano is one of my favourites, what do you think"?

Said Sid.

"Yeah, I'm enjoying it, he's really good I love his style, funny and intelligent, which makes for a bloody good read, which of his other books would you recommend then"?

Was her reply.

He thought for a moment before reeling of a number of titles, Cat's cradle, and slaughter house 5, being the two most significant to his mind and she made a mental note to look them up.

"So Sid, tell me what's your journey about today"?

Asked Lottie.

"I'm my way to a private viewing of an art show in London, as it happens, and you"?

Replied Sid.

"Me? Oh I've just got a free day and I thought I'd spend it in London maybe get some lunch take in a gallery or perhaps a museum or two, tell more about this private viewing you're going to"?

said Lottie.

"Oh, well actually it's my show, I'm an artist you see and I'm exhibiting a new series of portraits".

He said with what he hoped was nonchalant air.

"Oh wow"!

She exclaimed, before saying.

"That's so cool! I'd love to see it I'm a bit of an artist as well you see".

Sid smiled, of course she was, how could he possibly feel such a connection to someone without them having an artistic bent?

"You're certainly very welcome to come along, it's a private showing so I'll leave your name on the door".

Sid was pleased to be able to say.

"How wonderful, what time does it start"?

She asked.

"The doors open at three, but do come along a little earlier if you like"

Said Sid.

They spent the rest of the journey chatting until they parted, knowing they'd see each other again very soon.

3) The friend and mentor.

He'd been sat in the cafe browsing his paper for only a few minutes waiting for her to arrive, she had a tendency to be a little late for things but Sid had come expect this and tended to factor it in whenever they had a date, she'd asked him to meet her before the show was due to start and although he wasn't really sure why he was always happy to spend time in her company as they had over the years become great friends.

"Do you mind if I join you"?

He looked up from his newspaper at these words and there she was as lovely as she'd been at that first chance meeting in the Dumb Waiter all those years ago. with a smile he gestured to the seat opposite him.

"Please do".

He replied in their customary fashion.

"So what's all this about? I mean you're putting on a show in less than an hour".

He said checking his watch.

"I just wanted to see you before it all kicks off. I wanted to, well".

She paused briefly to reach inside her bag. Placing a gift wrapped package on the table she continued.

"Give you this, it's a gift to say thanks, you know, for all the help you and Emy have given me over the last few years, I wouldn't have gotten to where I am today without it".

Smiling he picked up the parcel.

"Thank you".

He said as he started to pull off the wrapper revealing a leather-bound A4 sketch pad, turning it over in his hands he noticed that the back had been embossed with the words.

"To Sid, the best friend and mentor a girl could wish for".

Smiling a little nervously with anticipation she met his gaze across the table.

"Do you like it, I had it made specially "?

63

He looked back up at her smilingly trying hard not let his eyes well up and give away just how touched he was by her gift.

"It's beautiful, thank you very much, I love it but you shouldn't have it must have cost a bomb"?

Was his replied.

"Well it's the least I could do for all your help, I couldn't have done it without you. Especially as you've been getting ready for your big exhibit in New York over the last couple of months".

She said.

They sat in silence for a moment. Easy in each other's company, as you'd expect two friends to be after a number of years acquaintance. The waitress came over and they ordered some drinks before their conversation resumed, Lottie spoke first.

"When exactly are you be leaving for the states"?

She asked.

"My flight leaves early the day after tomorrow, in the morning. I'll see off the last of the paintings later today, they're being shipping ahead of me so with any luck all I'll need to do when I arrive is see to the hanging etc, in the gallery when I get there. Then I'll be away for just about two months, while the exhibit runs ".

He said.

She sighed leaning back in her chair as the waitress brought over their drinks, she took a sip of her latte and said.

"I'll miss you, you know".

He smiled

"I'll miss you too, but I'll be back in time for the anniversary of the day we met in the Dumb waiter all those years ago so if we don't managed to get in touch before then let's set that date in stone for our next met up, what do you think"?

She nodded her head in agreement.

"Yes that sounds like a plan, let's say we'll meet at two o'clock?".

His broad smile showed his pleasure, as he said.

"OK that's a date. Come on then let's get over to the gallery your public awaits".

this said they finished off their coffees and left the cafe arm in arm.

4) The Anniversary.

She'd arrived a bit early, ten or so minutes before they were due to meet, So that just this once she'd be there when he arrived, Sid was never late you see, and she always was so she was determined to surprise him by getting there first. They hadn't seen each other since the opening of her London exhibit just over two months ago, which wasn't so unusual, they were both pretty busy people she herself had, almost straight after that first opening, which went down so well that she had quickly become the new darling of the art world, received an unexpected invitation to exhibit at a very fashionable and exclusive gallery in Vienna and as a consequence, had spent most of the last month or so flying between England and Austria in preparation and Sid himself had no doubt been very busy also.

She was eager to find out how his New York adventure had gone, she had heard the odd rumour that it had been a complete sell out, but had heard nothing from Sid himself. She checked her watch, it was already two fifteen and it really wasn't like him to be late at all. Only slightly worried she decided to give him a ring but his phone it seemed was currently unobtainable, so she gave up on that, deciding he was probably held up and considering all the times she'd been late for him she'd

65

just wait patiently until he arrived.

There was an abandoned copy of that days "Independent" on the table next to hers which she took up to see if anyone had done the crossword yet, while she was flicking through the paper looking for the puzzle page a headline in the arts section caught her eye.

Well known Brighton artist dies tragically.

Her heart skipped a beat and she suddenly she felt slightly sick, as she found herself reading the article.

In a tragic road accident involving a New York taxi and a bus carrying 25 passengers, Artist Sidney Keeler was killed driving to JFK airport on his way back to England after what critics called his greatest exhibit yet. The artist, renowned for his portraiture work. and the driver of the taxi were the only people involved in the incident to die with only few minor injuries and one hospitalisation received by others implicated in the collision. He leaves behind a wife Emily and two…..

Lottie could read no further as her eyes were welling up with tears, she suddenly thought to check her messages which she hadn't done since she returned from her last trip to Vienna, and sure enough there was a message from Emy Sid's wife of twenty-five years that she sent only that morning while Lottie must have been on her flight back from Austria. Leaving her coffee, grief-stricken and full of tears she staggered out of the dumb waiter that day never to return.

The End.

Jealousy

Called the green eyed monster,
The driver of deceit,
It's purpose is unclear to me?
And from it I retreat.

People seem to harbour it,
Dislike it does Imbue,
When worn as if it is a shield,
It festers in plain view,

No good can come of jealousy,
No favours will it do,
breeding little more than enmity,
Taking folly as its cue.

It makes you lose your senses,
It leads you to revenge,
Ugly at the best of times,
And always makes me cringe.

STEEL

68

* THE TONG: JAPANESE CRIME SYNDICATE

72

Nothing

I want to write something, about something, today and usually there's something in my head that can be 'transposed' (I think that may just be my word of the week) to the page, in one form or another.

Today though, there is nothing. There's no wry observations backing up, like they usually do. There's normally so much in there. Mostly they are pointless ponderings and mindless musings. All are noticeable right now, only by their absence. Today I have an empty head.

So, how will I handle this? What shall I write? I have, it seems, managed to write this much already just writing about having nothing to write.

"Nothing" is a strange word, most dictionaries define it something like this:

pronoun

- not anything; no single thing: *I said nothing, there's nothing you can do, they found nothing wrong*

- something of no importance or concern: *'What are you laughing at?' 'Oh, nothing, sir'* *they are nothing to him [as noun]: no longer could we be treated as nothings*

- (in calculations) no amount; nought.

adjective

[attributive] informal

- having no prospect of progress; of no value: *he had a series of nothing jobs*

adverb

- not at all: *a man who cared nothing for her, he looks* **nothing like** *the others*

- *[postpositive] North American informal* used to contradict something emphatically: *'This is a surprise.' 'Surprise nothing.'*

An absence of anything, what does that mean? It occurs to me that there is actually no such thing as nothing, it's impossible there is always something somewhere.

"What are you doing?"

"Oh, er? Well I'm doing nothing just sitting about relaxing."

Or

"Oh, nothing just admiring the day."

Or

"Oh, nothing just out for a walk."

Or

"Oh, nothing just watching (insert reality TV show here)."

Ok, fair enough, you caught me, that last one is as near to nothing as to make no odds but if you are just sitting, just thinking or just walking then these things are something, and yet it seems strange that they are referred to so readily as nothing.

There's usually so much in my head it's hard to decide what to do, this is quite a difficult condition under which to function and can cause a kind of hyper-stillness, or an excited paralysis.

Right now though, nope, my head is relatively empty. An empty head? What does that look like? here are some examples.

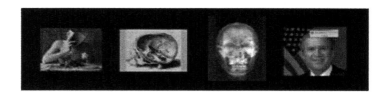

Nothing? The 5th century Greek philosopher Parmenides, of the Monist school, was one of the earliest western philosophers

74

to consider "Nothing" as a concept. Following a line of reasoning like this;

"To speak of a thing, one has to speak of a thing that exists. Since we can speak of a thing in the past, it must still exist (in some sense) now and from this concludes that there is no such thing as change. As a corollary, there can be no such things as *coming-into-being*, *passing-out-of-being* or *not-being*"

He argued that nothing *cannot exist.* because there is no change. Which if you ask me is just silly, change is all around us, day and night, the seasons, growth and ageing all show change.

The fact and circumstance of our own existence, our conception and birth, surely can be seen as a *coming-into-being* and our eventual death seems, to me, suspiciously like *passing-out-of-being* and either side of these two states, I reckon, is considerable as *not-being*. The idea of which long ago put paid, in my mind, to any fear of death itself I may of had as a youth. Logic seems to say, my state of existence after death would be just like it was before I was born. There's nothing in my mind here but the memories of learnt history, no actual memories of existence.

So in all probability, I, the entity here in referred to as the Klown, didn't exist. It seems only reasonable to assume it'll be the same once I die. This, to me, is a comforting Idea. I remember the first time I came across this idea in a quote from Samuel Clemens, better known as Mark Twain, who was a truly enlightened man. An atheist in a time when such things were virtually unheard of. He was once asked by a journalist if he feared death, which Mr. Clemens answered thusly.

"I do not fear death. I had been dead for billions and billions of years before I was born, and had not suffered the slightest inconvenience from it."

Changed my life those words did. Of course I'm not in any real hurry to die, and I still fear a painful death. The idea, though, that there is anything to fear but the loss of existence as a result of it is gone.

Parmenides was though, I think, right in one sense. There can be no nothing, not really. It wasn't until Aristotle, (384–322 BC) by distinguishing matter and space, space being a vessel where things, matter, are put, was a way out of Parmenides logical problem presented. Nothing, represented as the void, was just taken out of the equation.

The conceptualization of space came to its apex with Isaac Newton who propounded the existence of absolute space. Descartes, alternatively denied the existence of space. For him there was matter and it's extension, leaving no room for nothing.

From Hegel, to Heidegger on to Sartre, (who postulated two types of being, the first *être-en-soi,* is the harsh existence of being, something like a tree, a rock or a person might posses, the other, *être-pour-soi* or consciousness, which Sartre claims is nothing, as it can't be objectified and possesses no essence), and beyond.

Philosophers and thinkers have wrangled over the idea of nothing for centuries, and being philosophers, whose very existence depends, it seems, on being vague, they have come to no real conclusions.

What people understand as nothing varies dramatically from culture to culture, from east to west. Śūnyatā, which is actually more like emptiness than it is nothingness, the root of the word coming from *hollow,* is considered by many Buddhists to be a state of consciousness. A state that allows one to achieve *nothing* as a state of mind, allowing you to focus thought at a level of intensity inaccessible when consciously thinking. In some eastern philosophies nothingness is conceptualized as an ego-less state of being, that allows one to fully understand one's, place, however small that might be, in the cosmos.

In more recent times physics, more specifically quantum physics, has once more redefined our understanding of nothing. With experiments like the LHC, (Large Hadron Collider) demonstrating how elementary particles seem to pop in and out of nothing. As protons and lead nuclei race around at virtually the speed of light smashing into each other, the ensuing energy forces nothing to produce something. This has lead to the discovery, of the Higgs boson, which gives matter it's very mass, and now nothing seems even more unlikely. Giving us a universe filled with a quantum foam which even in the absence of anything else, matter or energy, is persistent throughout the universe.

Well as I started out with nothing to write about, I think I covered it pretty well? Thank you, once more, my dear non-readers, for your attention. Please return to your soup…

John Hegley's Shoes

I Listened to a man today.
And I didn't even have to pay.

It was a man quite specific.
Actually I think he's terrific.

John Hegley is his name.
Nobody is quite the same.

Funny, Specky, Geeky, Lanky.
Won't put up with any, hanky panky.

Like a spidery Rock a Billie,
Who's really more of a Billy that's silly.

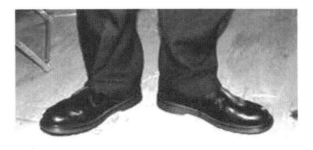

The What You Said Game

This is a little game to amuse yourself at social gatherings.

The rules are very simple, it goes like this, find someone to talk to. Go through the usual introductions the hellos and the name telling bit.

Once that's out of the way, you then start to repeat back whatever your chosen victim says to you, it's important to vary it a little, perhaps add a word at the beginning, or the end of your repeat,

fluctuate your tone to make it sound questioning, like Australians do with everything they say? Then just see how long it takes for them to notice.

With really self involved people, you can do it for ages without them noticing. I did it to this chap at a party once, and he didn't notice at all, I got bored, after an hour or so and just wandered off.

Please return to your soup.

The Bear and the Smilge

This is the story of the bear and the smoke dragon, also known as The Smilge.

You see my dear non-reader the Klown hasn't always been a clown, oh no, once there was the Gently Seeming Rainbow Bear who, in many ways, the Klown still is and will always be. It's like this you see, people come and go in our lives, some people you meet maybe only once and it can be a magical if fleeting occurrence.

Then there are those who you see, rarely but with whom it's always good. Some are loving and others still are just plain old good fun. However, sometimes, for various reasons, a relationship will endure. One such relationship is the one I share with The Smilge.

I was going to live in Italy, in the village of my father. Who is, obviously being from a village there Italian. When I first met The Smilge. I'd been there many times before, almost every year of my life untill the age of eighteen.

I had grown up being able to speak Italian, as well as the local dialect and had a not inconsiderable Italian influence throughout my life. But then I stopped going, preferring to stay behind. Leaving my sister and my parents to go on without me.

I'd have the most outrageous wild parties back at home, but that's another story, suffice to say I was having a high time and thoughts of Italian medieval mountain villages were, largely, far from my mind. Then one day I was at a party, well it was on the cusp of, during and after a party, chatting with a friend about life, love, art and just generally bonding. When talk turned to ideas of travel, about perhaps going on holiday together.

The last couple of times I had visited Italy had been without my parents and once with my friend, The Heavy Fish, aged sixteen, then again for a month with Wam the Beautiful and The Boatman, when I was eighteen.

So, the idea of doing so again with a friend didn't seem inconceivable and thinking that it might be quite a cheap way to go on holiday it was decided we should make all the arrangements and go in a few months when the summer arrived, I was about twenty at the time.

The summer came and went, along with any idea of this friend and I going anywhere, but the idea stayed in my head. I'd think about the idea of going over there from time to time, by myself, maybe find some work, be a bit arty and creative, and just generally to see how living there might be. After all my sister had already done it at least once or twice, for several months at a time.

I discussed the idea with my parents and it was agreed that I'd do it, so my mother sorted out my journey. She booked me passage on trains and boats. She had even arranged carriages and seat numbers and as she had gone to such trouble, I planned to follow the itinerary she had given me to the letter.

So It was shortly before my twenty-second birthday that I set off on my voyage of self discovery. It wasn't until I got to London and was walking along the platform beside my train to Dover that my itinerary following plan came a cropper. Each carriage had a Letter, starting at the beginning of the platform with 'A' then carrying on with every carriage in alphabetical order.

My seat was, according to my ticket, on carriage 'H'. So I walked down the platform, reading off each letter as I went, A, B, C, D, E, it was a long train, F, G, I. Hang on, I thought, it should be 'H' after 'G', I carried on walking to the next carriage, 'J', the next, 'K'. Mmmmmm? I thought and walked back up to carriage 'G'. After all it was always possible that I was a complete Idiot and 'H' came later still in the alphabet.

Not knowing what else to do, I boarded that carriage carriage 'G' to have a look around. It was a little while before the train was due to leave so there was only one person there, you guessed it, The Smilge. Beautiful and full of the excitement of travel she looked like she might be quite an approachable smoke dragon and I needed to verify just how idiotic I was so I said,

"Excuse me."

She looked up from whatever the book she was reading was, let's say it was the 'Blind Watchmaker' by Richard Dawkins, and said,

"Yes?"

I said, 'H' does come after 'G', doesn't it?'

She looked at me quizzically, and I could see further explanation was needed.

"In the alphabet, The letter 'H' comes after 'G', doesn't it?"

She considered me, and my strange question, for a moment, finally saying,

"Yes."

"So, if this is carriage 'G' where is carriage 'H', it's not the next carriage?"
I said, shrugging my shoulders to demonstrate my confusion. She thought for a moment more and suggested.

"Maybe it's further down the platform?"

So off I went in my bemused state, carrying on down the platform, and low and behold, there it was right after 'K', if I'd just carried on down the platform I'd have found it, and I may never have met The Smilge.

I boarded my carriage, found my seat and, settling in for my journey to the coast, started to listen to my Walkman.

The rest of the journey to Dover was relatively uneventful and passed without incident. Upon arrival at Dover I alighted and made my way to the bus that would take me to the ferry.
The Smilge did the same and we found ourselves sat next to each other on the bus. Well I say we found ourselves sat next to each other. What I really mean is she, being as I've already said a particularly beautiful smoke dragon, caught my eye again, and I'd liked her reaction to my probably quite odd sounding inquiry. So I deliberately sat next to her with the express intention of striking up a conversation.

This conversation was struck, and she turned out to be just about as interestingly good company as I hoped and we chatted about books, films, music, jam and life. We laughed and giggled.

Drank and ate, being generally good company for each other from Dover to Paris.

As it transpired she was inter-railing around Europe for a couple of months, intending to see much of what our continental cousins had to offer. Including Italy where she was due to meet her mother, who was to be holidaying in Florence at some time during The Smilge's journey.

So, I invited her to come and stay with me. If she should find herself anywhere near the village, she could look me up and come and visit, to which effect I furnished her with the address and a hastily drawn map so she would be able find her way relatively easily.

We parted company at Paris, and whilst I carried on for Italy, she went to visit Spain. I had another ten hours or so on the train until I would arrive at the station of Ventimiglia. The town closest to the village and after a restless night's sleep in a couchette bed, lying with a very fat snoring man above me and a Nun below, I arrived at my terminus and caught the early morning bus to the village.

I settled in, rekindled an old friendship or two, did a bit of work painting a bar, then as a waiter. Having grown up in the catering trade it was easy enough to find a job in a restaurant or two, as an extra waiter here and there up the valley. I'd been in Italy for about three weeks and was getting ready to go to the next village up the valley to work for the weekend.

I would start off at about eight or nine on the Saturday morning to get to work and not get back till midnight or later on the Sunday night Monday morning. It was the late afternoon early evening of the night before and I was about to have a shower, when, with only a towel around my waist. I heard a brummie voice shout up my stairs that she had found this girl, this smoke dragon, wandering about the village looking for me. It was of course The Smilge taking me up on my offer.

There she was bag on her back, with a curiously doubtful look on her face like I may have forgotten her or that perhaps I had changed my mind. This was of course not the case, and remembering how well we had gotten on I was obviously delighted to see her, she was very welcome, and I did my best to make her feel so. I showed her to her room, we chatted and drank tea for a while, and in the morning I went to work and left her to fend for herself, knowing instinctively I could trust her in my house during my absence.

I did my weekend's very hard work with my friend The Dark Light of the Enigmatic Cat, collected my wages and returned home to find The Smilge showered fed and rested.

Then something happened, who can say exactly what? But the two days she had intended to stay, turned into nearly two weeks, during which time we came to like each other, and so became good friends. We spent much time with, The Dark Light of the Enigmatic Cat, the three of us becoming almost inseparable, splashing in the river and playing in the sun.

It was about this time, after a couple of weeks, that she reminded me of her promise to meet her mother in Florence, and any way, she had already used over a month of her two month ticket and she had been to hardly any of the places she had planned to see. She said she would try to come back and visit again before she had to return home but that she could not promise she would. So The Cat and I, The Bear, waved The Smoke Dragon off, with a mixture of joy and sadness.

After she had gone the Cat was especially sad and he would talk about The Smilge often, asking The Bear whether or not she would return, and that if she did would he, The Bear, tell The Smilge how he had come to love her, in the tongue The Bear shared with The Smilge. That The Cat himself could barely keep a stiff upper lip in.

This worried The Bear because he and The Smilge had spoken often of love and companionship. Her expressing a desire to be free. To do as she wished, and to not get involved with people too deeply. As it came to pass she did return, after a little less than three weeks, and fun and frolics did ensue.

The Cat asked again for The Bear to express his feeling to The Smilge so with much trepidation the bear approached The Smilge and said.

"The Cat wanted me to tell you that he likes you."

To which she replied.

"Well, I like him."

The Bear wasn't sure he'd entirely gotten his point across, so he said.

"Yeah, well, he really likes you."

To which she replied once more.

"Yeah, and I really like him."

Feeling it necessary, for some bizarre masochistic reason, to really hammer his point across, The Bear said,

"Ok, but he likes you, like boys and girls sometimes like each other, more than just friends."

To which she said,

"So do I."

She eventually married The Cat, but it wasn't to be, and their story came to an end. The Smilge though? The Smilge still lives in the village. Twenty-one years later, now a woman smoke dragon, and has made a life there.

She lives with Two Smaller smoke dragons that she made herself on her pottery wheel. It is now, always has been and always will be, my pleasure to call her my friend. And that, my non-reader, is the story of the Gently Seeming Rainbow Bear and Smilge the Smoke Dragon. Please return to your soup.

Follow me

It all started one day when I was out for a walk in the woods. Out of nowhere the idea struck me that a walk in the woods might be a nice way to while away a few hours so I'd decided to grab a sketchpad and, as it was a very pleasant summer day, perhaps find some "woodlandscapes", as it were, to spend the afternoon drawing.

So there I was making my way, guided by varying spots of sunlight dapple, when there in front of me was a fox. He was sitting, the way they do, looking at me, but properly. You know with eye contact and everything. I stopped where I was and looked back at him. I was delighted, how often do you get to be so close to a real wild animal?

Anyway, we both just stood there, me moving very little, him seemingly disinterested, even occasionally looking away or sniffing the air, when out of nowhere, like a bolt out of the blue he spoke, that's right he spoke. He spoke, in fact, to me?!

"Follow me."

Is what he said, that fox. That wild animal that spoke to me. I was speechless which, with the benefit of hindsight, as I'm sure you can see was a strange and interesting juxtaposition of how it would usually come to pass between a human being and an animal. So there I was agog that this normally dumb animal had spoken to me, when he spoke again.

"Come on, follow me."

Was what he said, this time standing up as if ready to go. I couldn't believe my ears! A fox was talking to me how was this possible? Foxes don't talk? No animals talk!

He then trotted off, with one eye still on me as he went. For at least a moment I was rooted to the spot. Able to move all but my feet, I craned my neck, leaning around to get a better view of the path up ahead as there was a small bend. So as to see where the fox had walked to, but it was just out of sight. This caused me to lose my balance and trip over myself. I hit the dirt on my side cursing my clumsiness as I fell. Briefly the fox returned. Presumably to see what all the commotion was about. He stopped just after the little bend, sniffed the ground, looked about a bit, and then sighed.

"Get up, come on and follow me."

Was his next sentence. Then he turned around and once more trotted off down the path.
I quickly got to my feet and started to follow. Hesitantly and slowly at first, as he wandered off in front of me, glancing over his shoulder, as if checking to see if I was still there. We carried on like this walking through the woods, like a latter day little red riding hood and wolf, but sort of in reverse, for a little while. I couldn't believe what was happening, and felt myself beginning to doubt my own ears but still I followed.

It was then that, with another look over his shoulder, he left the path and made his way through the trees. So that now here we both were, following his own special path. Made up, no doubt, of a myriad of differing scent trails. We went deeper and deeper into the woods, so that the dapples of light that played across the woodland floor became more and more diluted.

We carried on this way for some time. Eventually the realisation dawned that I was almost certainly entirely lost. The fox, meanwhile, clearly knew where he was going. My mind was racing, what could this possibly all mean and more to the point where was I going? I had no Idea! The fox kept on, wending its way through the trees, taking detours around areas that, although clearly within his own ability to pass, would have been near impossible for me to traverse.

Eventually we came to a clearing where he stopped. Looking over his shoulder to check I was still there he moseyed over to a conveniently fallen tree, looked back at me and then to the log once more before moving off a way and sitting down. I took this to mean that this was where he wanted me to sit, so I did, placing the bag with my drawing stuff on the ground next to me. I'd been on my feet for quite a while so, as it happened, I was glad to have an excuse to rest them. Then he did it again.

"Wait here."

He said, once more speaking, like I wouldn't normally expect a fox to. Before striding off back in to the wood. I was perplexed, what was going on? Why had this strangely loquacious, at least for a fox, creature brought me to this clearing? I looked about a bit taking in my surroundings. The clearing was about twenty five foot across. Roughly circular and occupied by a number of logs made up of apparently randomly fallen trees, not unlike the one upon which I was seated, in a rough circle around the clearing. If you didn't know better you might even think they had been arranged that way. Behind me was a small stream of surprisingly clear water babbling away pleasantly.

The opening in the canopy allowed the summer sun to shine down, lighting up dancing dust motes in the air. It was, I have to say all very pleasant and I found myself thinking it wasn't a totally disagreeable place to find yourself on a sunny afternoon.
While I was looking around this break in the woodland, it started to seem rather familiar. I was struck by an intense feeling of deja vu. You know, as if I'd been there before. I was sure I hadn't though.

Presently the fox returned, this time though he wasn't alone. He was accompanied by two other foxes. One of whom was, roughly, the same size as the first and another who was slightly smaller. For some reason, I wasn't sure why, I took the smaller fox to be a vixen.

They walked over to where I was on my log and sat down in front of me. The first fox fixed his eyes on mine before saying.

"Who are you?"

I thought for a moment and then a moment more. Who am I? What sort of a question was that to be asked by a fox?

"What do you mean, who am I?”

I replied, a little taken aback.

"Do you know who you are?"

The fox retorted, a little impertinently I thought.

"Of course I know who I am."

I said perhaps a little tersely.

"Well then. Who are you?"

Said the fox, with more than a little exasperation in his voice.

"I'm... Well I'm, I'm?"

I said, realising that as it happened I wasn't sure? I racked my brains for an appropriate answer but there was nothing there? For the life of me I couldn't remember who I was? It was then that I found myself saying.

"I don't know! Why don't I know who I am?"

The fox looked at his companions, first the other Reynard and then the vixen, for a moment before sighing.

"It's happened again."

He said to his cohorts before returning his attention to me.

"We sensed that you'd forgotten and become stuck. It happens from time to time but don't worry, everything will be alright, which is why we called you here today. You need to return, at least for a short while, so that you can get your mind back."

I couldn't believe what I was hearing. What did he mean by I'd become stuck and needed to get my mind back? I had my mind I just couldn't remember my name was all. I just needed to think about it for a bit. It was bound to come back to me.

"What are you talking about. Forgotten what? What do you mean by I need to get my mind back?"

91

I said, the panic in my voice audibly rising as I spoke.

The lead fox sniffed the ground for a moment and looked around for a bit, as if collecting his thoughts.

"Look into my eyes."

He said, once more fixing his steely gaze on me.

I didn't want to look at him but I couldn't help myself. I found my eyes inexorably drawn to his. The world started to spin and blur. It felt like I was shrinking. Everything started to go dark, and I passed out.

I don't know how long I was out for but it was the gentle babble of the brook that brought me back to my senses. I found myself lying across the log with a bit of a headache. I looked up to see the others but something was different? There were still the four of us in the clearing, but where the vixen had been there was now a human woman. The Reynard who had met me on the path, what seemed like an age ago now, was gently licking my fur.

"Look into the water".

He said.

I turned my head and looked down into the stream and there looking back at me was a fox. Then I realised it was me, that was who I was. I turned back to look at the woman who returned my gaze and smiling, she knelt down and stroked my new glossy coat before picking up my bag and making her way out of the clearing, leaving the others to tend to me and I knew, just as he had said, that everything was going to be all right.

The End

Poem

I want to write a poem,
About what, do you think it should be?
I could, I suppose, throw down some words,
And see what I think it could mean?

You can start with commonly known phrases,
Or compose a soliloquy,
Be lyrical about faraway places,
Or use iambic pentametery.

Haikus are a type of poem,
Give them a go if you like,
Yes, this verse *is* one.

A poem can be about anything,
About good and bad and great,
There's a joy, about, which words can bring,
Not all rhymes though will come on a plate.

So if you'd like, to have a go.
Then a poem, you should write,
Writing verse is good to do,
So let your imagination, ignite.

Meme Tank: An aquarium of ideas

I like to think I'm a rational man, others may or may not agree, but nevertheless this is how *I see me*. I haven't always thought as I do mind you, as a younger man I gave truck to ideas that now I see as, although still of interest, ludicrous.

I like books and I've read quite a lot them. Tons of fiction and poetry, as well as a lot of non-fiction. Including more than a passing interest in science, in school initially, then in books ranging from 'A Brief history of Time' and 'The Ascent of Man' to name just two. Mostly these days I keep up with science by way of a magazine called 'New Scientist' which I'm going to consider as much the same as the reading of books as to make no difference, at least as far as the transfer of memes is concerned.

Also I have, it's fair to say, read and considered, even as reasonable from time to time, mostly in my past, a lot of the more esoteric types of literature. Covering such topics as, philosophy, religion, and all manner of mysticism. Taking in the likes of Alistair Crowley, Sigmund Freud, Wilhelm Reich, Karl Jung, Timothy Leary, Robert Anton Wilson, Aldous Huxley, Hume, Berkley, and Descartes, to name just some of the luminaries to whom I've given an interest. As well as reading books, like 'The Bible', 'The Koran', 'The Torah' the Tibetan and Egyptian books of the dead, Homer's 'Odyssey' and 'Iliad' and 'The Epic of Gilgamesh', in fact all manner of mythologies and legends, I've thought about gods and God, and pored over the words of many a great thinker.

The thing you notice, you see is, when you look at all this stuff, this grand human endeavour. When you really examine the products of this urge to explain all this input into ourselves, all this sensory data, "What the fuck is that all about?!" has been the collective cry, resounding throughout history. You inevitably find yourself seeing bits of it, that look an awful lot like other bits of it. You start to see all the archetypes of explanation gel together, telling similar if not identical stories.

Take for example the Egyptian gods, the Jewish patriarchs, and Chaldean kings. These three lists of names share striking correlations.

.

Egyptian gods	Jewish patriarchs	Chaldean kings
Ptah	Adam	Alorus
Ra	Seth	Alaparas
Su	Enos	Almelon
Seb	Cainan	Ammenon
Hosiris	Mahalaleel	Amegalarus
Set	Jared	Daonus
Hor	Enoch	Ædorachus
Tut	Methuselah	Amempsin
Ma	Lamech	Otiartes
Hor	Noah	Xisuthrus

These three lists of people seem to highlight different aspects of humanity. Let's take Enoch, for example, who was seen as a builder. He corresponds with both the Egyptian Hor and the Chaldean Ædorachus, both builders. In fact the builder motif comes up at least once more with the repeat of the seventh Egyptian god Hor, here comparable to Noah and Xisuthrus, both also builders, this time of boats. Another parallel between the three lists is that they are all, also, presented as lists of seven. You see these coincidences cropping up all over human history. Ideas that share, if not completely, the same themes, down to the beginning middle and end of stories, then elements written on different continents will correspond remarkably with each other.

A good example here is the flood Myth. Analysis, not mine obviously I've just read other people's, of some 600 individual flood traditions from across the globe, reveals a widespread concurrence on essential points: the prior corruption of mankind, a flood warning unheeded by the masses, a survival vessel, or high mountain where refuge is taken, the preservation of up to eight people with representative animal life, the sending forth of a bird to determine the suitability of re-merging land, significance in the rainbow, descent from a mountain, and the re-population of the whole earth from a single group of survivors. There are even more specific cases where names are uncannily close. Take the name Noah, which is especially remarkably persistent throughout the world.

Particularly so when you consider the ultimate language differences between peoples and the extreme local distortions which developed in flood legends. Yet the name seems to pop up as the hero in all of them virtually unchanged in such isolated places as Hawaii where he was called Nu-u, in the Sudanese myths we find Nuh, and in China Nu-Wah and his family found refuge atop a mountain. The Amazon region has Noa, in Phrygia it's Noe and among the Hottentots we have Noh and Hiagnoh.

You will often hear people citing Buddhist ideology's likeness to quantum mechanics. Or how akin the stories of Orsiris and the much later Jesus Christ are: they both conquer a devil, heal the sick and, in one coincidental meme, both raise the dead, but are these likenesses purely coincidental? Maybe not, perhaps they are simply the same stories gathering embellishment and variance with travel through space and time?

With examination you see how these memes might travel across oceans and continents, ideas and memes merging or simply consuming each other like badly matched fish in a tank, and this is what my thoughts are and how they are represented in my mind, as a vast glass tank, a meme tank, where I merge the ideas, imagining them as little families of strangely teated fish, see mother Judaism with her children Christianity and Islam, sucking at her breasts, Christianity herself has a litter of offspring feeding from her many nippled bosoms, Catholicism, Protestantism, Jehovah's Witness-ism, Quakerism, Mormonism, she's a profligate little meme that Christianity, with a host of little teat attachments gulping them down hungrily and excreting them as subtly different ideas, new memes born into my tank of meme soup.

I used to think of my Meme Tank as a guard against mistaking the map for the territory, that's what people do you see. They make these maps of life they use to get around the actual landscape of existence, which is at least, possibly, a little understood by us, though it remains largely unknown. This is basically what the maps are for, to fill in the large gaps left by what we don't know and often these maps serve us well. So well in fact that people tend to start to think, often developing this belief over hundreds of years, that the map is actually the territory itself.

Sometimes these cartographically led travellers will come across others with different maps, doing something in way that is different from theirs, and they might say something like.

"Hang on there, let's see your map?"

They might then look at the other map and notice that it is different from the one they have, so they'll say.

"Hey, your map's wrong!"

The other map users may in turn say something along the lines of.

"Really? Let's see yours?"

And of course they then see where that map is wrong, and will probably retort along the lines.

"Right, I see what's up here, it's your map that's wrong."

They might stand about awkwardly for a few moments before, inevitably, they fight.

Dangerous things maps, look at the wrong one, in the wrong place and you'll find yourself falling over a cliff or drowning in quicksand, but use the right map, in the right place, and you'll find you get most of the things you need: food, shelter, and all sorts of things will be laid at your feet happily, get it wrong, and they'll stab you.

Of course, now I realise that my meme tank itself is just a map, a useful tool for navigating life's highways and byways. It's a map that represents an approach to life I seldom take seriously anymore and if I've learnt anything from life then it's this: Taking yourself and your map seriously is a big mistake, leave that to other people. It's best and most fulfilling to make light of life. By which I don't mean be uncaring, or taking the pain, suffering and misfortune of others without due consideration. We still need empathy and understanding which is why it's still ok to take the piss out of people. Not too harshly and seldom to their face mind you.

Just remember that you are standing on a giant ball of rock that has been here for billions of years and will be here for billions more. You and I and our silly little maps will be here for merely a fraction of that so whatever else you find yourself having to do, try and have a little laugh now and again. Please return to your soup..

Mail Order Bride

James Derwent had always thought of himself as a regular sort of chap, he'd spent all his working life as a plumber living in Reading where he'd been born, and had lived ever since, for nearly forty years now. He wasn't rich, but as plumbers mostly do, he made a good living. He had his mates, he liked a pint and he supported his local football club. It was a simple life but, as I've already stated, he was a straight forward fellow, so, it was a life he liked.

Except, he was lonely. The one thing he'd not managed to date, was a successful relationship with a woman. He'd tried, god knows he'd tried. He'd even been married for a while. It hadn't worked out like he'd hoped. Women were rarely, if at all, how he thought they should be.

Julie, his ex-wife, had seemed, initially, to be OK. She'd acted as a woman should, she'd done the cleaning and cooking, as well as doing the other things you'd expect from a wife. Still, It hadn't taken long though, before things started to go wrong.

She'd do things like vacuuming while he was watching the footy, in fact that had been the cause of the *incident*. He'd been very reasonable really, three times he'd asked her to stop, she'd just carried on, saying,

"I'll be done in a minute".

If only she'd just done as he'd told her, if she had, he was sure his slight irritation wouldn't have escalated into anger. But she'd just carried on blissfully unaware of how annoying she was being, so he'd hit her. He got up out of his chair and slapped her clean across the face and told her to turn off the Hoover, sit down, and wait for the match to finish.

Well, it had all gone downhill from there really. One month later she was gone, he'd got home from work to find all her stuff, clothes, shoes and her little nic nacs (every cloud has a silver lining) were missing, and he never saw her again.

He'd heard from someone down the pub a few years later that she'd been seen living with a bloke somewhere in Norfolk, shortly after that the divorce papers turned up. He didn't even bother to read them, he just signed them and put them back in the post.

The truth of the matter was, you see, that James was a bit of an anachronism, to him sexism and women's lib where dirty words.

99

He'd been brought up, in a very male dominated environment, his dad was the head of the household and everybody, his mother included, did as they were told or they got *the back of his hand*. A woman should know her place, and if she didn't then it was his job to show her. *I mean, he would think regularly, what kind of a world is it where a man couldn't give his woman a little slap every now and then? You know, just to keep her in line. To show her who's boss.*

There'd been a few other woman since then, but it was always the same. They either didn't want to clean up after him, or they couldn't cook. One girl who stayed over after the second or third date, he couldn't remember which, even refused to iron a shirt for him, what kind of a start to a relationship was that, saying *no* to the first thing he'd asked her to do? As it was she'd had to do it in tears.

She never came back and on top of that she'd gone to the police! They'd turned up on his doorstep the very next day, two police officers, one a man the other a woman, which, obviously shocked James a little, but he kept it to himself and invited them both in. Escorting the officers into the lounge, he went to the kitchen and made them all a cup of tea. He spent thirty minutes or so explaining that he'd hit her by accident stretching his arms out quickly whilst yawning and he denied asking her to iron a shirt. He didn't think they'd believed him but as he hadn't actually bruised or marked her it was her word against his. So, he'd had to accept a stern talking to about bullying, been given an *unofficial* warning, and that was the end of it.

Mind you, that whole ordeal had put him right off the entire idea of relationships and women, consequently he hired a cleaning lady and told himself he just didn't need a woman, after all, he could afford to see a prostitute from time to time if the desire arose. He put all ideas of companionship to the back of his mind and threw himself into his work. It wasn't as if he was lonely, he had loads of mates, well, he knew everyone down the pub at least, and there was Derek, his drinking buddy, he'd be fine on his own, who needed women anyway?

"I need a woman Derek!"

Said James after drunkenly ordering another round of drinks, "It's just all this women's lib stuff, it does my head in, I want a woman like they used to be," he went on, "One who knows her place, someone who'll do my cleaning or iron my shirts, without giving me any lip."

He took a long slug on his fifth pint.

"You won't find a woman like that,"

Replied Derek.

"At least not in this country,"

He continued. James had a large gulp of ale and slowly a thought started to form in his alcohol soaked mind.

"Yeah, that's right, you've got it!"

Slightly surprised, but quite pleased that he may of gotten something right, Derek perked up a little.

"Really, how's that then?!"

He said.

"I need a foreign woman, one from a place where they breed them nice and compliant, like..?"

He struggled to think in his addled condition, finally coming up with.

"Thailand!"

Making Derek jump a little, spilling, much to his consternation, a drop or two of beer.

"Yeah, Thailand, those Oriental birds are gorgeous, and they respect their husbands."

This all seemed to stir a memory in Derek's similarly addled brain.

"Do you remember Greg?" Said Derek.

James Thought for a moment, a moment admittedly longer than a sober man would have needed.

"Greg who?"

He eventually enquired.

"You know, Greg, Greg Simpson?"

Offered Derek

"Oh, Greg, Greg Simpson."

Agreed James, still not really sure who this Greg character was, but keen for Derek to move on with what he had to say about this as yet unidentified person.

"What about him?"

He asked.

"He got himself one of those mail order brides, and as it happens, she came from Thailand."

Derek continued.

"I saw them in town a week or so back, he seemed really happy, they've got a kid and everything."

At the suggestion of children James baulked a little.

"Oh no, I don't want any kids, I don't like kids, they just annoy me."

He said.

"Well, you don't have to, find one that doesn't want kids, you're paying after all." Derek replied.

James took a long swallow of his pint, finishing the last quarter in one gulp, finally bringing his glass down on to the bar with a drunken thump.

"It's your round Derek, and I need a piss."

This said he made his way, staggering only slightly, through the busy bar over to the gents. Returning a few minutes later, hands unwashed, to find a fresh pint dutifully ordered by Derek, awaiting him in front of his stool at the bar.

After a few silent moments of solid drinking James picked up the thread of their conversation and asked.

"So, where do you find these *mail order brides*?"

Derek thought for a moment or two, trying to remember a conversion about it his brother-in-law had told Derek he had had with Greg's sister, Derek having never really discussed it with Greg himself.

"It was a web site he went on, yeah, that's right, he found her on some web site, did all the arranging, you know visas and stuff, he had to fly out there a couple of times I think, spend some time with her, meet her family and that, and now they live over in Calcot."

Said Derek.

James's foot slipped from the bar between his stool's legs where it had been resting. He only stopped himself from completely falling off his stool and collapsing on the floor by gripping onto the bar and righting himself, not before spilling a substantial amount of his beer.

"Don't want to have to go to Thailand, do you have to go to Thailand?"

He suddenly came out with.

"I think you do, yeah, I think that's part of the deal, so her family can meet you, I think?"

Said Derek uncertainly.

"Oh!" Said James and carried on with his pint.

The next day was Sunday, which started with the usual hangover. James had nothing on that day so he rolled out of bed late morning and spent the rest of it nursing a sore head in front of the telly, with lots of water and Alka-Seltzer. After watching nothing in particular on the box for a while his mind started to wander back to his conversation with Derek about mail order brides the night before. It was all a bit hazy, he barely remembered leaving the pub and getting home, god they'd been smashed, but he remembered this other chap Derek had spoken of.

Whose name he'd already forgotten, that had found his wife on the internet.

Not that he was taking it all seriously, he wasn't flying half way around the world to find a woman. If they couldn't come to him they could forget it! Still, here he was hung-over, alone, sat in his underpants and dressing gown, on the verge of another lonely wank, and after all he was quite curious and those Thai girls are gorgeous, what harm could it do just to take a look at the internet.

He turned on his computer, then went in the kitchen to make some coffee while it booted up. Returning with a mug of hot steaming Colombian blend, and some toast, he took his place at the computer and opened internet explorer. It didn't take long for him to google up a plethora of sites advertising the availability of woman from places as far reaching as Russia to East Asia. Actually James had always been fascinated by Oriental looking women. They struck him as exotic and glamorous, not to mention their reputation for being loyal and compliant wives. That was all he wanted, it wasn't that much to ask was it?

He examined a number of the sites google presented him with, and although there were some beautiful women looking for husbands over here. It seemed a visit to their homeland was always involved. He hadn't even been to France. He didn't have a passport, he'd never bothered to get one, why should he? He wasn't going anywhere so he was hardly going to go jetting off around the world for a bird, however pretty she was.

That was it then, might as well get dressed and go down the pub for some lunch. He was about to turn off the computer, when a pop-up appeared on his desktop with the words;

"Thai Brides over here dot com, East Asian girls already living in England looking for husbands."

With a link to a website thaibridesoverhere.com. James was immediately intrigued, and hit the link, it was, from what he could make out, essentially an introduction agency for East Asia women, living in England and English men who wanted to meet up with a view to marriage. They had an office in London he'd have to visit, but he wouldn't have to leave the country. He Immediately signed himself up. He filled out an extensive questionnaire then, after a little browse through the women on the site, he found one or two girls he liked the look of and added them to his favourites. Before getting dressed and going to get his lunch, all the while, with a little wry smile on his face.

It was a few days later when the e-mail arrived. It was from the appropriately named Ernest Matchman who had been assigned as James' personal introduction co-ordinator. It further explained how Thaibridesoverhere.com was not in any way to be considered a dating site, it was, in fact, a serious introduction agency for Thai women already settled and living in this country looking to meet English men with a view to a committed relationship and marriage. It went on to say that all introductions would be arranged through Ernest and an initial meeting would take place at their London offices. He asked James to e-mail a reply so they could arrange a date for Ernest to come to visit him in Reading for a preliminary meeting. Just so he could get to know James a little better and to discuss exactly what James was looking for in a woman. James sent a brief but polite reply, detailing the sort of times it would be convenient for Ernest to pay a visit, and over the next couple of days, following the resultant e-mail exchange, a meeting for the next weekend was organized.

James opened the door to find a very smartly dressed man who, although obviously in his late fifties, would still be considered handsome, with a big smile on his face. He stretched out his arm, offering his hand and asked.

"James Derwent?"

Offering his hand in return, James said.

"Yes, that's me, you must be Ernest, please come in."

They shook hands, firmly and vigorously, before James showed Ernest into the living room. Ernest took a place on the couch in front of the glass-topped coffee table and James settled into his usual easy chair, across from him. Placing it on the coffee table, Ernest opened his brief case and took out a couple of folders, presumably containing files, a note book, and a pen. These he placed on top of the closed case, which he used as if it were a makeshift desk. Opening one of the folders he ran his eye over James' questionnaire before putting it back down and saying.

"So James, it's a pleasure to meet you, and I must say judging by your answers to the questionnaire you seem like just the kind of man, we're looking for. I'd just like to ask a few questions of my own so I can gauge how best we can help you."

"Sure fire away."

said James, eager to get the process moving.

"OK, so how long, roughly, have you been single?"

Was Ernest's first question.

"Oh, now you're asking, fuck, how long has it been?"

Said James, and after only a little thought he came up with.

"Let me see, it must be four, or maybe, five years, I guess?"

Ernest made a note of James' answer in his note book, before asking.

"And roughly how many relationships have you had to date?"

James thought for a moment more.

"Not many, two or three, what I would consider to be significant relationships, including a brief marriage and a few very short-lived flings."

He answered a few more questions in a similar vein, before Ernest put down his note book and picked up the other folder.

"Now, in here I've got files on some of the women we represent, including the ones you added to your favourites on the web site, as well as some that have already shown an interest in you."

"Oh, really?"

Said James, obviously quite pleased by the idea that interest had been taken in him, and why shouldn't there have been, *after all, I'm a bit of a catch*, he thought to himself. Ernest laid the files out on the coffee table as though he was croupier spreading a deck of cards atop a blackjack table. Each file had a photo of a very beautiful Thai woman paper clipped to its top right corner, and although they were all striking girls there was one that particularly caught James' eye. She had long dark hair that seemed to shine out of the photo, and bright blue piercing eyes that appeared to cut right down to his soul. James didn't know about love at first sight but lust? That was clearly in evidence. Crossing his legs he pointed to her file.

"Who's she?"

He asked looking up to see Ernest smiling broadly.

"Ah Kanya,"

Replied Ernest, as he leant across to pick up her file.

"Yes, she is lovely, and she was one of the first to favourite your profile,"

He went on.

"Would you like to meet her?"

Enquired Ernest.

"Yes, yes, I would love to meet her."
Was James' eager reply.

Ernest opened his brief case again and took out a diary, and after a brief flick through its pages said.

"OK then, well, how about a week today? That would fit in very nicely with my schedule and give me time to make all the arrangements for your introduction."

107

Not wanting to be outdone James collected his appointment book, from his computer desk and checked his own schedule.

"Yes, that should be fine."

"Good, I'll sort it all out then I'll e-mail you to confirm the time and date when I get back to the office."

This said Ernest got some papers out of James' case folder and offered him a pen.

"This is our standard contract it basically explains the payment structure and covers liability, standard stuff."

James hesitated for a moment, then thinking 'what the hell!' signed on the line.

This done Ernest put his things back in his case, minus Kanya's file and James' copy of the contract. He stood up extending his hand once more, this time though, it wasn't empty but contained a small plastic jar with a screw lid and a medical sticker. James took the jar from Ernest's hand curiously and, fearing he knew the answer, asked.

"What's this for?"

"Ah, yes said Ernest our company has a strict no drugs policy so I'm obliged to ask you for a urine sample before I leave."

James looked at Ernest incredulously. for a moment before asking,

"Are you serious?"

Ernest nodded his head in confirmation, saying,

"You can of course refuse, in which case our business will end here and you will incur no cost whatsoever."

Ernest offered his hand for James to return the specimen jar. James looked at the little jar for a moment thinking, *what did it matter to him, a little splash of piss?*

"OK, Give me a minute,"

He said. He went upstairs to the bathroom returning a few minutes later with a just under half-full jar of his own urine. Ernest took the jar and popped it first into a sealable plastic bag before placing it in his case. Then, offering James his hand one last time, he said,

"Thank you for your time James, it's been a pleasure and I look forward to seeing you in London next weekend."

After shaking hands for a last time, James saw his guest to the door and watched as he drove away. Closing the door he returned to the lounge, sat down, and picked up his potential new bride's file. He could hardly believe how beautiful she was, a man could so easily lose himself in those eyes, he couldn't wait to meet her.

A week of work and trips to the pub passed as it usually does and before he knew it he was on the train to London, dressed in his best suit and full of tense excitement.

It was raining when he got off the train, so he hurried to the tube station where he bought a cheap umbrella from a news kiosk and made his way to the underground. The offices of Thai brides over here were situated in a building, smaller than he'd expected, in Islington, not far from the tube station. He pushed the button on the intercom and waited.

After a few seconds the door was buzzed open and, after briefly shaking the rain from his brolly, he entered a small but plush reception area. A, not surprisingly, beautiful Thai girl sat behind a desk looked up at him expectantly with her best receptionist's smile.

"Hello sir my name is Chiang, how can I help you today?"

She said in perfect English.

"I'm James Derwent, I've got an appointment to see Ernest Matchman for an introduction."

Chiang ran her finger down a list of appointments before she found his name.

"Ah, yes Mr Derwent, if you'd like to take a seat I'll let Mr Matchman know you're here."

She gestured towards a small area set aside for clients to sit and wait. He sat down in one of the chairs in front of a small table scattered with a few magazines. It wasn't long before Chiang answered the phone, she spoke briefly, in what, James assumed was Thai, and told him he could go right up, pointing towards a small lift door in the far wall.

"You need floor six,"

She said as he entered the lift.

He smiled a thank you and hit the button, the doors closed and James waited for the feeling of upward motion you normally get in lifts. Strangely it didn't happen, and few moments later the lift opened onto a room with some plush looking sofas, a cabinet, and a large window that looked out over the city. Not knowing quite what to do with himself, James made his way over to the window, to take in the view. It wasn't raining anymore and in the short time he'd been in the building the sun had come out and was shining over London. *Must have just been a bit of a shower,* he thought before making himself comfortable on the largest of the sofas. Then a door he hadn't noticed next to the lift opened. Out walked Ernest with, what James hoped was Kanya, walking head bowed behind him. James stood up to greet the new arrivals offering his hand to the approaching duo. Ernest took his hand with his usual broad smile and said.

"James, good to see you welcome, to our offices,"

Before he stepped to one side to introduce the lovely young, clearly subservient, girl behind him.

"This is Kanya, Kanya this is James."

She raised her head to reveal those piercing blue eyes and her shining smile.

"Please to meet you Mr Derwent."

110

For more than a moment James was dumbstruck, overcome by her beauty, she was very beautiful indeed. Her skin looked soft and smooth and James imagined what it must be like to touch her. It was Ernest who broke the silence.

"Shall we sit down?"

He said gesturing for Kanya to take a place next to James and they all took a seat, Ernest sitting on the smallest of the sofas. It was Kanya who spoke first.

"Would you care for a drink Mr. Derwent?"

"Oh, erm? Please call me James."

He said a little taken aback by her formality.

"And yes I'd love one, I've not had anything to drink since a horrible coffee on the train."

"OK, James, well we've got tea or coffee if you like, or I can get you something stronger, if you'd prefer?"

"I'd murder for a beer!"

He said hopefully. His gaze followed her, barely able to take his eyes way, captured as they were by her radiant beauty, out of her seat to get his beer from the cabinet, which revealed itself to be a small fridge full of bottles. Taking one out she poured it into a glass she took from the top of the cabinet and handed it to him, she did the same for Ernest, before resuming her place on the sofa.

"Well, what do you think James, would you like to see more of Kanya?"

Asked Ernest. James looked over at him, his eyes and mouth wide open, as if coming out of a trance before he spoke.

"Oh yes, definitely."

He replied eager to get intimate with this woman.

111

"OK, then," replied Ernest, "First things first, Did you bring the cheque?"

James reached into his inside pocket taking out a check for the sum that had been agreed in their e-mail exchange, five hundred and fifty pounds which, apparently, was to cover admin fees as well as being the first part of his payment for the introduction itself, a further two thousand pounds would be required before the process was over, and passed it to Ernest who placed it in his pocket.

"Right well I'll let you two get know each other, I've got a couple of other appointments to see to this afternoon, just buzz the intercom when you're ready to leave."

He stood up leaving his unfinished beer, and once more offered his hand, which James took and shook gratefully before Ernest left them alone.

That first afternoon in each other's company flew by as they chatted about everything and nothing, James gaining more and more confidence as it became increasingly apparent just how deferential Kanya was, which, he had to be honest, was turning him on enormously. Twice more that afternoon she poured him a fresh beer on top of offering him delicious Thai food she had prepared, as well as other refreshments, all of which he'd accepted happily.

He smiled languorously to himself all the way home on the train and that night his dreams were full of her and her beautiful eyes.

The next day James received two more e-mails one from Kanya saying how much she'd enjoyed meeting him and how she very much looked forward to seeing him again, and another from Ernest with a proposed courting plan, which, he was at pains to point out, wasn't a strict agenda to be followed but more about working out what was convenient and best for both him and Kanya.

James made more visits to London in the ensuing weeks, all of which, it seemed, turned into dates. They'd spent a day site seeing in the city as well as going out for dinner a few times, Culminating in a night of intimacy, their first, in a hotel one night after James missed his last train home, and what a night it had been! James had never known a woman to be so focused on his pleasure, he had left to go back to Reading the next morning in a haze of satisfaction he'd not previously thought possible.

They always seemed to meet at that Islington office, and it never even occurred to James to wonder why this would be so, or where she might live herself, wrapped up in the excitement of it all as he was. Eventually she started to visit him in Reading and he pretty much stopped going down to London.

It was after her fifth visit to Reading and after they had been seeing each other for several weeks that James, while they were out having dinning at a local Italian restaurant, suggested she move in. She'd been a little shocked by the idea, and said that she couldn't, which kind of surprised James, as he'd been fairly she sure she'd say yes. Of course he asked her why not?

"I want a husband James, I can't just move in with you without at least the commitment of an engagement."

Upon hearing this James got straight down on one knee and proposed there and then in the restaurant.

"Kanya, I love you and I want you to be my wife."

Overjoyed, she'd accepted immediately. She stayed that night, and, as far as James was concerned they had the best sex he'd ever had. Kanya moved in a few days later and James immediately changed his Facebook relationship status to *engaged*.

A few days after she moved in James got a phone call from Ernest, ostensibly to offer his congratulations but also to offer the company's help in organising the wedding.

"It's all part of the package James,"

He said.

"We give a comprehensive service you see, following our clients' progress until we're sure everybody is happy."

Ernest continued.

"And, how much more is this going to cost me Ernest? Bearing in mind I've already paid you somewhere in the region of a two and a half grand, all of which I'd like to add I was glad to pay, as, after all, I am very happy with Kanya."

113

Said James with slight suspicion in his voice.

"Oh don't worry James, when I say it's all part of the package, that's what I mean, it's all already paid for. We have our own facilities as well as an in-house registrar who performs all of our weddings, you leave it all to me, have the two of you decided on a date yet?"

Hearing that he wouldn't have to fork out on wedding expenses certainly appealed to James' sense of the frugal.

"All included you say?"

"That's right James. Of course the reason we can supply this as part of the service is because we do, like I said, do it all, in-house, of course that does mean you will have to seriously limit the number of guests to just a few friends and family,"

Replied Ernest.

"Well that's OK, I don't really have any family to speak of, both my parents are dead and I'm an only child, it was going to be pretty much just my mate Derek as the best man."

Said James.

"That's fine, all I need now is a date, and I can start sorting everything out. Did you have one in mind?"

Asked Ernest.

"We haven't decided yet, I was thinking maybe early in the summer?"

Suggested James.

"The summer you say, Mmmmm?"

Ruminated Ernest.

"That's quite a few months away, any reason, you'd want to leave it so long?"

114

He went on.

"Well no, not really, I just thought it might be nice to have, you know, a bit of an engagement. What do you think then?"
Replied James.

"Well now, let me see," Ernest said, prior to going quiet for a moment while, James assumed,

He checked a diary, before saying.

"It's February now, early summer is going to mean a wait of four or five months before the ceremony, is there really any reason to leave it that long?"

James thought for a moment before saying.

"I suppose not, when would you suggest?"

Ernest ummed and ahhed for a little while and then said,

"Let's see, we have got a free Saturday coming up in a couple of months, April the seventh, how does that sound?"

There was silence at the other end of the line while James considered Ernest's proposal. He had a point, why delay the wedding, he wasn't getting any younger, and Kanya was everything he could of hoped for. she cooked she cleaned, and every morning he had an ironed shirt, and the sex, oh the sex.

"Sure why not."

Said James.

"Marvellous, I'll go ahead and make all the arrangements,"

Said Ernest. It was all happening so fast, it had been only, what, six or seven weeks since they'd met. If you'd have asked James, all those weeks ago, if he thought he'd be married to his dream girl before the current year was even half way through. He would of just laughed at you, but here he was, only couple of months from what he believed would be the happiest day of his life.

It wasn't at all like his previous wedding to Julie. There had been months of planning and stuff to do for that. Admittedly he hadn't really contributed to the preparations at all, he'd just paid for everything. Julie and her family, which was huge, had organised all the details, but still, it had seemed to drag on and on and when the day finally came round it was all a little odd. An entire half of the church had been taken up by her massively extended family. It made James' side seem pitiful by comparison. He'd managed to scrape together a handful of mates who took up just two tables at the reception, which he'd hated. He felt like the price for marrying their daughter had been to basically pay for all of her family to get pissed. Ten and a half thousand pounds that wedding had cost him, and for what? She'd left after a few months!

This time it would be different, they'd been living together for a couple of weeks now and he felt like a king in his own home. He didn't have to lift a finger, his dinner was always ready, and always delicious. His clothes were always clean and put away. The cleaner hadn't been very happy when he'd given her a week's notice, he was, though, very happy not to have to spend the three hundred odd pounds a month he paid her.

Every evening when he got home, either from work, or the pub, she was ready with his slippers and a drink, a beer or a whisky, if it was straight from work, a cup of tea if it was from the pub. And the sex! Oh god it just got better and better, she just seemed to know how he liked to be touched, he'd never known such ecstasy, he'd no idea how she did it, and frankly he didn't care, so long as she didn't stop.

It was raining again when the fateful day came, and they decided to take the train. He wore his best suit and Kanya wore a beautiful oriental style dress called, she'd told him, a *Cheongsam: i*t was silver with lotus flower embroidery. James decided that, as he was going to be his best man anyway Derek might as well travel down with them on the train, and so the three of them set off for London.

By the time they arrived in the city the rain was coming down hard, so they got a taxi from the station to the Islington offices where the wedding was to be held. Ernest was in the lobby to meet them when they got there and the four of them only just fitted in the lift up to the sixth floor.

116

The lift opened onto the room where James had first met Kanya, and Ernest asked them to wait here while he disappeared through another door, this time in the far wall that James also hadn't noticed the other times he visited, to see if everything was ready.

Kanya dutifully poured both the men a beer. She and James sat down while Derek had a little wander about taking in his surroundings.

He made his way over to the large window, which gave an almost panoramic view of London, noting only briefly that, in the short time it had taken them to enter the building and come up in the lift, the rain had stopped.

It was then that Ernest reappeared and bid them follow him through the door. They followed him into another longer room, this room too had a large window, also with a sunny view out over London. There were a dozen or so chairs, set out like you'd expect, in rows with a space down the middle like an isle leading to a tastefully dressed desk at which sat a plump friendly looking woman in an Armani suit. Opposite her were four chairs, the outer two already occupied by two people who would be introduced to James and his little entourage as Mary Beestock and Harry Jones. They were to be the witnesses, really only there to sign the marriage certificate, and they were both very pleasant, wishing the happy couple well et cetera. *They really had thought of everything* mused James as he walked with his, very soon to be, bride to take their places for the ceremony ahead.

It didn't take very long, The plump registrar, whose name was Bridget, introduced herself and the witnesses before she handed James and Kanya both a laminated A4 sheet each, on which where some pre-written vows, she briefly explained what would happen and started. The official text was as you'd expect, lots of:

"In the sight of those here present ..."

And the appropriate amount of:

"In the eyes of the law."

As well as some:

"To love and to cherish ..."

It all sounded like fairly standard stuff, James and Kanya dutifully read their parts, his were highlighted in blue and hers in red, until the registrar said,

"I now pronounce you husband and wife, you may kiss the bride."

Which he did, feeling like he must be the happiest man in the world.

His happiness continued over the coming months and Kanya persisted with her attentive behaviour, encouraging James to become more and more dependent on her, causing him to start doing less and less for himself.

"Have you put on weight?"

Asked Derek one night down the pub.

"A little."

Replied James.
"It's good living you see Derek, and contentment."

He went on.

"Good living and contentment."

James repeated wistfully, and continued.

"It's wonderful, I tell you Derek, I've never been so happy, she really looks after me, and her cooking, my good she can cook anything. Every evening it's like I've got a top restaurant in my house, and she never complains, if I come in late and a little tipsy, for example, and the sex, god, she fucks like a crazy woman, and it's all about me, my pleasure always comes first."

Derek just smiled and tapped the top of his glass, slightly drunkenly, glad for his friend's new found happiness, and hoping that this would spur his generosity. James dutifully and happily ordered another round.

The next morning had been a Monday and james was looking at himself in the mirror thinking about his size. He was getting quite big, with a not insubstantial spare tyre around his middle and his face had become a lot rounder. It wouldn't be long before he'd have to buy some new trousers, he'd only just managed to button his jeans. He went to the bathroom and before he brushed his teeth he noticed his bathroom scales. It had been months since he weighed himself, so on a whim he stood on the scales to see just how much weight he'd actually put on.

He had one of those slight shock moments that make you feel a little dizzy when he saw just how big he'd become, he'd put on almost a stone and a half in weight, *fuck me*! he thought.

He went down stairs to find Kanya in the kitchen preparing his breakfast, his usual fry up. He sat down at the table and she placed a plate of food in front of him, piled high with bacon, eggs, sausages, beans, fried potatoes, black pudding, fried mushrooms and fried bread, which was becoming a bit of a ritual, and then went to the sink to do the washing up.

"Kanya," said James.

"Yes darling?"

She asked.

"Do you think I'm getting fat?"

Kanya paused her washing up briefly, prior to turning to say.

"I think you are handsome, it is good for a man to carry some weight, it is very masculine,"

She sat down beside him and removed her rubber gloves before she continued,

"It makes me happy to see that you enjoy your food, you do enjoy the meals I cook for you?"

She tilted her head slightly, with a certain coquettish concern that made his heart melt.

119

"Of course I do darling, your cooking is wonderful, I'm just wondering if I'm having too much of it, I don't want you to think I'm fat and ugly, just because I'm a man it does mean I don't like to be thought of as attractive."

She leant over to him, taking his face in her hands, she brought her face to his until their lips touched in a passionate kiss. After a lingering moment she pulled away and said,

"I think you are a very handsome man and that it suits you, to be big, it shows that you are a strong man, who can take care of his wife."

This said she went back to her washing up, leaving him to finish his breakfast, worrying about his weight had spoilt his appetite a little so he didn't eat it all, and kissing her goodbye he left for work.

Even though he believed what Kanya had told him regarding how she felt about the way he looked, his weight still preyed on his mind a little, so he decided to start going to the gym again. He used to go rather a lot but hadn't for quite some time, it must have been four or five years, it had been so long that his membership had lapsed and he'd needed to rejoin. A few months passed and although he hadn't really lost much weight, neither had he put any on, and anyway, now that he was working out at least a couple of times a week he was bound to be putting on some muscle bulk, which would balance out all the hard work and the apparent lack of corresponding weight loss.

It was a few more weeks before James noticed he was in actual fact still putting on weight, so he decided to go and see the doctor. The net result of which was a two hour session with a nutritionalist and a diet plan, which he dutifully took home for Kanya to implement, which she did, mostly, aside from the odd treat, stick to.

Funny things people, they like to think they're clever and they sometimes are. Often people prove themselves to be great manipulators able to inspire others to move mountains, but as it's only ever other people they can manipulate, that in turn means they can be manipulated, and easily.
Take James, here we have a prime example of how a man's idea of love can be shaped by his upbringing, his father was brought up with

what's known as a *traditional morality* which nowadays would be seen as misogynist bullying clap trap. There was a male head of the family and everyone, including Mrs Derwent, abided by his rules, if you didn't you were beaten, that was how you learnt. But if these now bizarre seeming rules where adhered to then everyone was happy and James' dad had no need to discipline anyone.

There's no excuse for James' behaviour towards the women in his life but there is a reason, he believed things should be a certain way, and now that they were he was happy, he hadn't hit Kanya once in all the time he'd known her. He was content, at ease with life, and he continued to put on weight.

They'd been married for about eighteen months, when one Sunday afternoon, whilst watching the match with his feet up and a beer, James started to feel a dull pain in his side. He was considerably larger now weighing in at an impressive nineteen and a half stone and as a *larger* man he was inclined to get the odd achy pain from time to time, so he ignored it and carried on watching the match. The pain persisted over the course of the match, gradually getting worse. Until the game finished, by which time it was getting quite bad. He thought it might be indigestion and he knew there were some indigestion tablets in the bathroom cabinet.

Kanya was out shopping so he'd have to go and get them himself. He made his way heavily up the stairs pausing occasionally to double up with cramp. Eventually he made it to the bathroom. Now in some considerable agony, he opened the bathroom cabinet and fumbled about with its contents until he located the indigestion tablets. Crunching a handful up in his mouth and swallowing them down with a gulp of tap water straight from the faucet.

He went into the bedroom and laid down on the bed with his arms tight into his body. He curled up in a foetal position on the bed and started moaning in agony, hoping that Kanya would return soon to help him. He stayed there unable to do anything in the face of the extraordinary pain that seemed to wrack his body now, for half an hour, before she eventually came back. Hearing his agonised cries from downstairs, she ran straight up to the bedroom and was right by his side. Taking his head in her hands, she said,

"James, can you hear me?"

He just about managed a strained nod through the pain.

121

"What's the matter darling?"

She asked with concern in her voice.

"I'm in so much pain, everywhere hurts,"

He replied through clenched teeth.

She stroked his head and thought for a moment or two, she nodded to herself and coming to a decision said.

"It's started, honey. Don't worry, wait here, it'll all be over soon, I'll go and speak to Ernest."

After kissing his now very hot and sweaty forehead ,she left the room.

What had she meant, *it's started* what had started, and why was she going to call Ernest and not a doctor? Why was he in so much pain? He felt as though his skin was going to burst, the pressure on his chest was making it hard to breathe and he was almost paralysed, curled up in a sweaty ball in the middle of the bed. Then he noticed the door.
A door had appeared out of nowhere in the wall and what was more, it was the outside wall. There was nothing on the other side of that wall but empty air, and through the pain, James found himself thinking, *What the fuck is that*? He looked at it a little closer, and now he came to think about it, he realised there was something familiar about the door. Then it hit him, it was just like the door to the lift at the thaibridesoverhere.com's offices in Islington.
It was all bizarre enough to distract James from his pain slightly and he stared at it with a surprised and slightly confused expression on his face. After only a few seconds the door slid open to reveal Ernest wearing his broadest friendliest smile. He stepped out of the lift into the room. The lift closing and then just disappearing as if it had never been there at all, behind him. He walked over to the bed and sitting on the edge, he patted James on the shoulder and said.

"How are you feeling old chap?"

To which, still wracked with pain, James said,

"What the fuck is going on?"

Through clenched teeth, grinding against the enormous agony, he repeated,

"What the fuck is going on?"

At that point Kanya returned to the room and took up a place on the other side of the bed from Ernest.

"How is he doing?"

She asked Ernest.

"He's fine, it'll all be over soon."

He replied.

Hearing this last from Mr Matchman, James managed to spit out,

"What will be over?"

Ernest looked over to Kanya questioningly, which prompted her to say.

"He may as well know the truth now, after all it's so close to the end."

Kanya cradled James' head in her arm and using a tissue from the box beside the bed mopped his very wet brow with her free hand. Ernest stood and had a pace about to collect his thoughts, before he started to speak.

"I'm not really called Ernest Matchman, James."

He paused to allow James to take this in, before going on.

"I'm not even human."

He said.

123

James managed very weakly to say.

"You're fucking crazy."

Ernest laughed a little and smilingly said.

"No James, I'm not crazy. I am from a far distant part of the galaxy. My people have long been able to travel to distant stars and have technology far in advance of this world's."

James just stared at Ernest. Shock acted as an anaesthetic and he momentarily forgot his agonies. Ernest was talking like a crazy man! From a *distant part of the galaxy*? *From the funny farm more like!* Ernest continued.

"My race are a nomadic people, we travel the stars going from planet to planet as part of our breeding cycle. You see the gestation of our young requires a certain hormone to allow our progeny to come to term. Right here on this planet, that hormone is available in abundance."

Ernest paused once more to marshal his thoughts, before asking James.

"Do you remember when we first met, James and you gave me a urine sample?"

James nodded remembering how he'd thought it was a bit odd at the time. Ernest continued.

"It wasn't to test for drugs, it was to test your testosterone levels, and I know how highly the males of your species prize these things so you'll be pleased to know yours was particularly high, very *manly* indeed, I'm sure."

James started to obtain a certain tolerance to the pain, helping him to gather his thoughts enough for him to say.

"What's happening to me?"

Ernest looked over to Kanya.

"Would you like to tell him my dear?"

Kanya looked down at James' face, sighed and began.

"Every time we've had sex, over the months we've been living together, I've impregnated you with one of my eggs, they've been using you as a host taking your testosterone to fuel their gestation."

She paused for a moment, to allow him to fully grasp what that actually meant. He tried to work it out in his head, and failed. They'd had sex hundreds, maybe thousands of times. That did, though, account for his massive weight gain, and would mean he had god knows how many alien eggs inside him. He was struck by an overwhelming sense of panic, his heart started to race, what could he do?! This was crazy, was the Earth being invaded by aliens? Surely not, he must've become involved in some kind of crazy space cult, or something? Not to mention that his whole body was now an explosion of pain, as if every nerve was being tortured individually.

"But you look human!"

Said James, every word a new triumph over the pain.

"We are what you might call shape shifters. We have the ability to physically alter our appearance to resemble other species. This is how we have so easily infiltrated so many other worlds,"

Said Kanya, who was still gently stroking his head. The pain became overwhelming once more.

"Oh god! Why am I in so much pain?"

Screamed James. This time Ernest addressed his enquiry.

"They're hatching, inside you now, and as each one hatches it starts a period of rapid growth quadrupling in size in a matter of minutes, until, soon after, they leave your body to take up places in the incubation chambers on our ship orbiting above."

"So I'm going to give birth?"

Asked James, still not believing all of this. He imagined they'd poisoned, or drugged him somehow, maybe in his beer?

"Well, if by *give birth* you mean, burst open as our rapidly growing young eat their way out of your body? Then yes, I suppose you are."

James screamed as the pain mounted anew, he felt his every fibre aching with an intensity he'd never previously experienced. His torso started to expand as the tiny creatures inside him grew and grew. The skin of his ballooning belly became so taught that the hundreds of tiny forms could just be made out subdermally. Sweat was now streaming from his body, the bed and bedclothes where drenched. James started to twitch and jerk, unable to speak he screamed, his mind raced. Could all this be true?
It was all so crazy, but the pain, oh god the pain. At first the split in his belly was small, then it ruptured with a loud ripping tearing noise and hundreds of tiny creatures swarmed out of his body. This was the last thing he saw, and just before the swarm reached his mouth, he managed a final scream of,

"Fuck me!"

The alien young had the look of bipedal insects with large abdomens and a substantial set of teeth and sharp claws allowing them to make short shrift of James' body. Leaving no more than a few blood stains and a wet bed. Suddenly, Kanya and Ernest began to stretch and jerk, their bodies twisting and deforming until they resembled larger human sized versions of the tiny aliens who, now they had finished their first meal, started to cling to the two adults and each other. Allowing them to be carried through the newly appeared lift door in James' bedroom wall, and away.

It was four days before anyone even knew James was missing. Derek had found the house empty. He'd been curious as to why James hadn't been to the pub lately, so he'd popped over to James', maybe he was ill or something and Derek might be able to help. When he'd got there, the backdoor was open so he'd gone in calling out James' name but, for obvious reasons unknown to Derek, no one had answered. And of course neither James' nor Kanya's body were ever found.

Epilogue:
"You can go up now Mr Miller,"

Said Chiang from her desk as she gestured towards the small lift doors in the far wall of the small reception area of the offices of thaibridesoverhere.com.

"Thank you,"

Said the man seated a little nervously, in the reception area, across from Chiang. Simon Miller, an insurance salesman from Bromley, loved East Asian girls and he smiled admiringly at the beautiful Asian receptionist. He was a regular kind of guy in most respects, not bad looking, admittedly his hair was receding a little now he was getting into his thirties, but he was fit, healthy, and he exercised regularly. His problem wasn't his looks, no, his actual problems were twofold one;
He was chronically shy, he could not for the life of him talk to a woman without stuttering and mixing up his words, and two;
He was scared of flying, he'd tried god knows he'd tried. One time, they'd had to abort a take off to allow him to get off the plane before it flew, after a particularly physical panic attack. He entered the lift and as instructed by Chiang, he hit button six. The doors closed and a few moments later slid open to reveal a room with some plush looking sofas a cabinet, and a large window that looked out over the city.
He looked about a bit, finally making his way over to the window, which showed a clear sunny bright day in the city below. *It's cleared up a little since I got here,* he thought remembering the grey clouds that had been hanging in the sky when he arrived.

Imagine, for a moment, that you could fly through the window like a virtual camera and you fly right through it. Finding yourself on the other side but once through, the city you saw before has gone and instead you find yourself surrounded by a holographic field projection. Projecting a steady repeating image of London to the eyes of anyone stood in front of the window in that room.

You, in turn, fly through this technical mirage, finding yourself all of a sudden hanging high above the Earth, floating in space, you turn around and look back at where you think the building Mr Miller and before him James had believed they were in should have been. To find it has gone, along with the illusion of London. Replaced by a giant spaceship orbiting high above the Earth. The Earth that Simon

127

Miller had just been matter transported up from, taking his first steps towards wedded bliss.

.

The end.

Meaning

Meaning isn't inherently,
Nor externally to be found,
Fallacious quests and journeys,
all about us though abound.

They lay about a cloudiness,
That obscures the truth from eyes,
Mind maps, the mistaken realities,
Lie in dogmas many ties.

Isis is the life bringer,
Halos hang around,
Eris brings us chaos,
Anunake, come on down.

Eucharistically are cannibal,
All consuming of the flesh,
By wheat-cakes of Osiris,
It seems that we are blessed.

Upon a stone of destiny,
sceptre in the hand,
Pretending to divinity,
Lest humanity not be found.

Consciousness explains a soul,
A concept over thought,
The mind can see above the fog,
If answers true are sought.

From stars is all constructed,
All things and minds or men,
Explained by way periodically,
Elemental now as then.

No Meaning will you find outside,
though vainly they have tried,
Instead seek through community,
So easily will you abide.

An Alternative

Look on the book shelf of almost any person with power, be they captain of industry, general, president or prime minister and you are very likely to see a copy of *Niccolo Machiavelli's* The Prince.

Machiavelli himself was a Fifteenth Century diplomat about whom little is known until he was appointed to the post of second chancellor and then a little later the secretary, to the Republic of Florence. He had a fairly active and influential political life. Until, that is, the Medici returned to Florence after forcing Piero Soderini into exile in 1512. As a result of this change of power Machiavelli found himself being tried for conspiracy which led to a year of imprisonment and torture.

It was soon after his release that Machiavelli decided to write the Prince (although it wasn't given that title until sometime later Machiavelli referred to it as his *Pamphlet*) The Prince itself isn't a large book but it is considered by some to be one of the earliest works of modern political philosophy. Although some see it as, and aguably Machiavelli meant it to be, a political satire that exposes tyranny and promotes republicanism.

However you see it, you can't deny it's influence on people with power throughout its six hundred year history and you will often hear politicians, generals and CEO's alike citing it as such.

Many think the book itself was a reaction to the trauma of his ordeal at the hands of the Medici. He hoped that Cosimo Di Medici would eventually read it, though it's unlikely that he did.

The book itself is basically a manual on how to get and keep power and it doesn't pussyfoot around either. It tells us that *it is much safer to be feared than loved because ...love is preserved by the link of obligation which, owing to the baseness of men, is broken at every opportunity for their advantage; but fear preserves you by a dread of punishment which never fails* and, that *If an injury has to be done to a man it should be so severe that his vengeance need not be feared*. It's from this work that we derive the word *Machiavellian* to describe someone who is devious and deceitful. It is also, if somewhat inaccurately, cited as the source of the phrase *The ends justify the means*.

It is an interesting book; It's brief, well written, even witty and tinged with irony. If you want to understand the real truth of how the politics of governance work, even to this day, then you should read it.

I read it as a young man and have always found it interesting that a piece, which is in essence, a fifteenth century man's effort to deal with the trauma of an extended period of torture, so ably exposes the inequities of the way the modern world is run.

Here's another phrase, this time from a man called *John Emerich Edward Dalberg Acton*, The nineteenth century Catholic Historian and moralist, *Power corrupts and absolute power corrupts absolutely*. The actual quote is a much less general statement and goes like this, *Power tends to corrupt, and absolute power corrupts absolutely. Great men are almost always bad men*. This is the problem, to gain power in today's world it is necessary to be *Machiavellian*, to lie and cheat. To become a leader you must allow yourself to become, if you are not already, corrupted, or under a current political status quo that exists around the world, you will lose your power.

So essentially if you seek power whether it be for noble or ignoble ends the very power you seek will corrupt you.

What does this mean? Well, I think it means that all political systems that depend on people seeking power are fundamentally flawed and will always end up with small a percentage of people, or an elite, holding all the power while the vast majority of people, albeit to varying degrees, are kept oppressed and ignorant. Which is why generally speaking revolution tends to replace elitism and oppression with other only subtly different forms of elitism and oppression.

You often read and hear in the media about people like, for example, Russell Brand, calling for revolution, people not to vote and an end to political elitism. It is increasingly apparent that if we want to live in a world where people are treated with fairness and equality then the way we find the people who run things has to change.

So what's the alternative? You rarely, if ever, hear anyone suggesting anything that would actually be an alternative, so what can we do? How do we remove the desire for power from the equation?

I've been giving it some thought and I've got an idea, now bear with me as it's a little on the radical side.

I think what is needed is to do away with the vote.

"What."

I hear you cry.

"The vote is the corner stone of democracy."

Is it, is it really? Samuel Langhorne Clemens, better known as Mark Twain a man, if you ask me, well before his time is often quoted as having said "If voting made a difference it'd be illegal."
And he's right as is the aforementioned Mr. Brand, your vote is, to all intents and purposes, pointless. It makes you feel like you have some power but that power is all but an illusion.

I live in England where we have three main political parties, the Conservatives, Labour and the Liberal Democrats. The latter party being the one I've followed since I was allowed to vote and the truth of the matter is there's little to choose between them these days. The existing political landscape of this county is little more that a homogenous mass. Purporting to differing political ideologies with little that actually tells them apart and people are, if only subconsciously, becoming aware of this. Which is, I believe, why so few people actually use their vote anyway.

In the last UK general election (2010 at the time of writing) just fifteen percent of the population turned out to vote, which means that eighty five percent of the people in this country didn't vote, for not only the current coalition between the Conservatives and the Liberals but any government at all.

How can that be right, how can people have been driven to such an apathetic approach to their only method of deciding their own fates? Is it because few people have any faith in it? Probably.

It's not just the vote though, that we need to do away with. Party politics, this has to go as well. I think it's this that really causes the elitism, that idea, that I'm right and you're wrong. That seems, more often than not, to lead to an over inflated sense of entitlement in the elitist.

"Because I'm right I deserve more than you and you are wrong and anyway I come from a long line of people with a greater entitlement so nur!"

OK, I realise that's over simplifying it a little maybe but you get my point.

Right we've done away with party politics and voting, what now, how will we get stuff done and who is going to do it all? The answer is we will.

"How" I hear you ask yet again. "Are we going to do that if we don't vote for someone or other"?

We use a system like they use to choose jurors for trials. It can't be that complicated to sort out. The electoral register, instead of being used to give people a vote is used to choose, out of everybody, representatives from a given geographical area. We could even call that area a constituency. Not just one person though, maybe a dozen perhaps, or maybe even more. (Let's say thirty for the sake of this scheme, I'm an ideas man after all it's up to someone else to work out the fine details). Who would then be compelled to give up their jobs and form a local council. They will have the right to return to their jobs after their five year period if they so choose. In fact I imagine an entire new industry developing, where people are employed to work in place of the people who've been obliged to give up their jobs to go into government, again, fine details yuck!.

They would all be selected randomly from every walk of life; they could be of a liberal bent or a conservative one. They could even be a Marxist absolutely anyone at all could be chosen. Well I say anyone, I suppose there would have to be conditions that would exempt and exclude some, people already found to be corrupt convicted felons, perhaps people with extreme mental disabilities.

They then decide between them who will represent their body as local area council representatives nationally, say three or four of their number. Who will then become whatever it is we decide to call what we replace MPs with. Obviously the council members would have to vote for the councils national reps (hey let's call them that, CNRs, brilliant!) So we wouldn't be getting rid of voting entirely, just making it so that less people vote in a fairer way.

133

These few are then sent to what I'm going to randomly call, the *Senate*. We would then have another, this time semi-random, selection process. Where out of this senate people are chosen to populate different senate departments, according to the skills they already possess. For example teachers would be picked to work at the department of education, doctors and nurses at the department of health and so on.

That way people who know about the thing they are running will be running it. Then you won't get a man who's never taught anyone, like Michael Gove trying to decide how people should be taught, instead you have people who know about such things doing it, makes sense right?

You could even go a step further and have one more body that's roughly equivalent to the cabinet, which would be there mostly to coordinate stuff like a committee.

Hey let's call that one the National Coordination Committee or NCC, which would be made up of representatives from all the different departments who choose a chairperson between them (again fine details, not my strong point).

So that's it basically, governance by random'ish selection. It might just be a stupidly unworkable idea, and I am certain many will say it is but hey, it's an alternative. Please return to your soup.

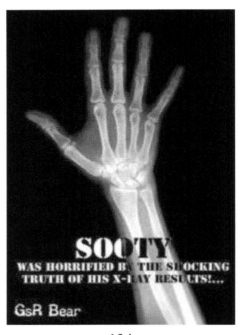

SOOTY
WAS HORRIFIED BY THE SHOCKING TRUTH OF HIS X-RAY RESULTS!...

GsR Bear

134

Normally I'm Weird

Normal is a funny word,
So speaking relatively,
Being safely placed amid the herd,
or just in the vicinity?

Weird is what you call me,
That's fine I understand.
Is it really what you think I am,
Or just a handy way to brand?

Oddly placed upon the world,
Always labeled as distinct,
Creativity unfurled,
A thinker on the brink.

Am I really on my own,
Or are we all the same?
Am I all I want to be,
Or am I as I came?

Normal's not a word I use,
Others wear it as a sigil,
There's need to neither to win nor lose,
When considered as individuals.

The Strange Way Some People Move Through Your Consciousness

I was watching the Telly recently. When I saw a promo for the Brit Awards, and who should I spy playing a mature Scissor Sister but the one and only Mr. Paul Lavers.

This put me in mind of the first time Mr. Lavers entered my consciousness. I was very young and I didn't really know it was Paul. It was the late 70's , 1978 I later learned, and I was a boy of ten living in Norfolk, Kings Lynn, I settled down to watch my weekly dose of Dr Who, this particular episode was called. 'The Androids of Tara'. Enter Farrah the Swordsman, played by the inimitable Paul Lavers and what a fine swashbuckling figure he was.

The years passed, I forgot about Paul Lavers.

Telly evolved, and wonder of wonders! In my late teens, I must have been sixteen or seventeen at the time. The biggest thing since Channel 4 happened, through the night television. In my case "Anglia through the night". Presented my Mr. Midnight himself, Paul Lavers. Over the next several or so years I spend many an early morning in the company of Paul.

It was around this time that a friend and I when for a night out in Norwich, a nearby big town. We ended up at a night club called Hy's. and who should be there in the flesh? You guess it Mr. Lavers, out with a young lady, presumably his wife.

My friend had spent the odd early morning with me and the telly. So he was aware of who Paul was. We didn't approach him. But it was a highlight of our evening. You don't see many celebs in Norfolk. So it stuck in my memory.

Well the years passed, I grew up proper like, did some stuff, travelled worked etc.

136

Eventually I settled in Brighton. Working as an animator, writing painting, generally being creative, and occasionally seeing Paul on QVC.

After a few years in Brighton a friend of mine moved to Norwich, following a job. So I went to visit him for the weekend. It must have been around 2001, 2002, or there about's.

That weekend we went for a stroll around the town, bit of trip down memory lane for me. When we came upon the place where Hy's used to be. So I told my friend of my Paul Lavers related experiences and I remembered Paul again.

The weekend passed and late Sunday night early Monday morning I drove down the M11 heading for the south and eventually Brighton. After about an hour or so, I stopped at the Birchanger Green services, for a coffee to perk me up for the rest of my drive.

I got my coffee and a cake, found myself a table and settled in the read. As I looked up to from my book, who should I see wandering over to the table next to mine? That's right, Mr. Paul Lavers. Accompanied by a colleague. They sat down next to me we exchanged nods, and after a lull in their conversation I said

"you're Paul Lavers aren't you?"

He said he was indeed Paul Lavers, and we chatted for about an hour, exchanged business cards and I drove back to Brighton thinking about the strange way some people move through your consciousness.

You can find out more about Paul at his web site.
http://www.paullavers.com

I Gatecrashed Al Pacino's Party

No really I did, I gate crashed Al Pacino's Party. Was that a collective gasp I heard from my non readers?

I promise it's so completely true, slightly bizarre but absolutely for real. I never had to go to Hollywood or Paris or even London In fact I didn't even have to leave my home town of Kings Lynn in Norfolk (which, sadly, I have to admit if only for the sake of this story, is my home town). Why on earth would Al Pacino have a party in a provincial arse end of nowhere, semi industrial East Anglian town?
Isn't it obvious? He was making a movie, the Movie in question was "Revolution" which, as the name suggests, was about the American Revolution. The town of Kings Lynn, you see, in the early 80's was more like New York harbour was in the 18th century, than New York harbour was in the early 80's. Which doesn't say much for Lynn in the 80's it's come on a bit now and is less 18th century than it was. So Al Pacino and a host of others came to town.

I was an extra in the film as were a whole host of people I knew, You don't see me in it mind you, as I never made it to screen. I did however sit next to Annie Lennox, who complained about her aching feet, I had a puff on Donald Sutherland's Pipe, Graham Greene the Native American Actor famous, most recently, for appearing Twilight sequel "New Moon" told me he liked my hair, as he tussled it on more than one occasion. David Bailey told me to get out of the way, oh and, one of the cast of the children's television programme, *Grange Hill*, offered me a line of speed in their hotel room. The irony being they were a leading light in the Grange Hill "Just say No" to drugs campaign.

So how did it come about that I went to Al Pacino's party? Well I've always been a quite friendly likable kind of chap, and it's not been so unusual, during my life, for people to take a shine to me, and over the years many and sundry have. I don't Imagine the fact that I wasn't half bad looking in those days didn't help bit.

I ended up, as a result of my friendly demeanour, winning charm, boyish good looks, and possibly most importantly "local Knowledge", hanging out with a load of the younger more minor actors. Like Melissa

Wilks and Sid Owen, in the hotel they were all staying at. The dukes head I believe it was.

One or two other names that stick in my head are: Sam Smart and Martin Murphy, I got on with these two chaps very well, even keeping in touch with Martin for a time afterwards, I wonder where they are now? As well as a chap called Joe Wright. Oh and how, could I forget my very good friend Warren Saire, the making of whose acquaintance is a story in itself. So there I was hobnobbing with all these actory types which, at the kind indulgence of my parents who allowed me the time off work from the family owned restaurant to play at being a bit thespy. It all made for a few weeks of great ego building fun.

Like all good things it did eventually come to an end, and on the last day of filming the lead actor, the aforementioned Mr. Pacino, decided to throw a party in a local Restaurant called the "River Side Rooms" for the cast and crew.

Being neither cast nor crew, I wasn't invited. But being a rambunctious young fellow I decided to go anyway, to which end I teamed up with a couple of chaps who had come up from Portsmouth on an enormous boat, one of the biggest props I've ever seen, as stunt extras. They had similarly endeared themselves to the younger cast members. Though their names escape me, I do remember the name of the rat that accompanied one of them, he was called Mr. Rat. We initially decided to try the direct approach. The restaurant was attached to a theatre and art gallery which was all behind a quite large gate that led through to a kind of patio area that they would use for outside dinning, in the brief time during summer when this was possible. We approached the gates, where there were two rather large gentleman who looked like they would have been happier wearing a track suit and gym shoes, rather than the suits they'd been squeezed into, we gave our names, rather hopelessly, and they checked their list.

It was absolutely the only time in my life anyone has said to me "you're not on the list"

"We may not be on the list" said my rat accompanied companion, "but surely Mr. Rat is?" Shockingly he wasn't on the list either.

So with the certain knowledge that once in, we'd be safe in our cloud of favoured minor celebs, we set out to find another way.

139

Being the one with the "local knowledge" it was really down to me to find that way.

The Riverside Rooms, as the name suggests, was right beside a river, the River Great Ouse to be precise. I'd eaten there once or twice before with my family. and I thought it may be possible to get in if we got down on to the river bank, as the tide was out. To see if we could find a way in by climbing up the wall that separated it from the water.

This entailed a stealthy creep over one or two private gardens, and then a climb down to the river bank. which as it turned out was a good few feet down, let's say thirty, for the sake of argument and because it sounds quite dramatic. We then had to walk along the side of the river till we got to where the restaurant was. We looked up, it was very high, maybe more than thirty feet, but fortune as ever favoured the bold, and an enormous marquee had been erected in the patio area I mentioned earlier. Which was secured by these huge ropes that stretched the many feet down to the river bank.

Using these ropes we were able to climb up and slip, unseen by security, under the side of the marquee and enter as if we were bona fide party guests. We soon found our friends and in no time at all were enjoying the party, and how cool was it, there where all these famous people Hugh Hudson, the director, I remember seeing Steven Berkoff, Dexter Fletcher and Sid Owen to name but four. Even Al himself was there for a bit; wearing what seemed to be big white pajamas.

The food was a buffet that had been flown in from the restaurant of the Roux brothers in Paris, Imagine that! The drinks were free as were cigars and cigarettes and I drank smoked and ate merrily all night. At one point I found myself sat at a table next to a gorgeous woman, who looked a little, well, bored I suppose, she must have been a little older than me, I was seventeen at the time, I reckoned her to be at least in her twenties maybe twenty five or so. Any way she was gorgeous and, being of a mind to chat to lovely ladies, I struck up a conversion with her.

We exchanged names and she informed me people usually called her Tasha. We talked mostly about nothing really just making observations about the party, "look at the that funny drunker than us person", style comments. We seemed to be keeping each other

140

amused, quite ably, she laughed and gave me friendly body language all, it seemed, was going well.

Then we needed new drinks, and being the consummate gentleman I volunteered to go to the bar and get them.

Once at the bar I discover, very drunk, one of my fellow gatecrashers, the one with Mr. Rat.

"How are you doing over there?" He asked.

"Oh, very well" Was my only slightly less drunken reply.

"Do you know who she is?" he said

"Yeah, she said her names Tasha, and she one of the actresses on the film" Said I.

"She's Natasha Kinski" he informed me.

I then realised she was really rather famous, and not just an ordinary lovely German sounding actress working on the film. I of course knew there was such an actress, I'd seen her dad Klaus in both "For a Few Dollars More" and The 1979 remake of "Nosferatu" and I knew even that she was in this very film, but I'd never seen her in anything before. Therefore I didn't know her face.
I'd thought I was chatting to a relatively regular person. I returned to the table where she was sitting, but the knowledge I now had, caused me to become not a little star stuck and I lost it, so she soon lost interest, became bored and I think, even left the party.

Still I had a great time and it went on till the early hours of the morning. They finally kicked us all out and I had some time to kill till the next bus home, so me, and my fellow crashers went back to this gay guy Steve's place. Steve was a local chap hired as driver on the film and so was by virtue of this crew and therefore had been invited to the party.

I knew him from around town, so felt safe enough going back to his. Once there I passed out on a couch. I'm not sure how long I'd been passed out, when I was awoken by some slurping noises. I opened my eyes to something I'd never seen before.

On the other couch Steve, who actually later became quite a close friend, was giving one of the guys a blow job whilst wanking the other one off. I didn't go back to sleep. I waited till everyone was snoring and asleep and left quietly, and a little wiser.

I went home to bed and had erotic dreams about Natasha Kinski.

The End

The End of the Book

Thank you for reading this book. In case you're interested in other stuff by GSR Bear and the Kosmic Klown. Then there are a couple of places online where you can see animations, sketches and films that they've made using the web addresses below.

https://vimeo.com/channels/kosmicklowntv

As a suggestion for something to view on Vimeo try the short film;

Room 4 Rent

Also there's around sixty videos on YouTube that can be found here.

https://www.youtube.com/user/PietroGLantrua

So just at the end the real name is revealed.

thanks for coming.

Please return to your soup.

Last but by no means least, I want to thank my friend.

Sally McCorry

Who made good the spelling and grammar. In fact this is the bonly tit she didnt speelcheek.

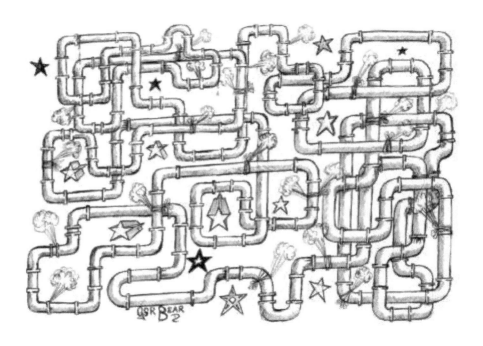

144

Printed in Poland
by Amazon Fulfillment
Poland Sp. z o.o., Wrocław

64301578R00083